THE CHRISTMAS CATCH

By
Ginny Baird

Published by
Winter Wedding Press

Copyright 2012
Ginny Baird
Trade Paperback
ISBN 978-0-9858225-3-8

All Rights Reserved
No portions of this work may be reproduced
without express permission of the author.
Characters in this book are fiction and figments of
the author's imagination.

Edited by Martha Trachtenberg
Cover by Dar Albert

About the Author

From the time that she could talk, romance author Ginny Baird was making up stories, much to the delight -- and consternation -- of her family and friends. By grade school, she'd turned that inclination into a talent, whereby her teacher allowed her to write and produce plays, rather than write boring book reports. Ginny continued writing throughout college, where she contributed articles to her literary campus weekly, then later pursued a career managing international projects with the US State Department.

Ginny's held an assortment of jobs, including school teacher, freelance fashion model, and greeting card writer, and has published more than ten works of fiction and optioned nine screenplays. She's additionally published short stories, nonfiction and poetry, and admits to being a true romantic at heart.

Ginny is the author of bestselling novels *The Sometime Bride* and *Real Romance*, and has just launched her "Girls on the Go" series, which premiered with *Santa Fe Fortune*. She's a member of Romance Writers of America (RWA), the RWA Published Authors Network (PAN), and the RWA Published Authors Special Interest Chapter (PASIC).

When she's not writing, Ginny enjoys cooking, biking and spending time with her family in Tidewater, Virginia. She loves hearing from her readers by email at GinnyBairdRomance@gmail.com and welcome visitors to her website at http://www.ginnybairdromance.com.

THE CHRISTMAS CATCH

John turned his attention on Tyler, waiting eagerly nearby.

"Ever been on a toboggan, young man?"

Tyler shook his head.

"Well then, you're in for a treat. Hop on!" he instructed, positioning Tyler right behind Mason. Tyler promptly wrapped his arms around the dog, who leaned back to lick his face.

"Will he be all right?" Christine asked with concern.

"Sure. You'll be right behind him, holding on."

"And where will you be?"

"I'll be hanging on to you." John grinned and her heart melted.

Christine warned herself not to get carried away. It was just an outing in the country. But when John settled in behind her and snuggled her and little Tyler securely in his arms, she couldn't help but blush in his embrace. He was so strong and capable. Though the steep slope ahead looked formidable, Christine had no qualms about her and Tyler heading down it with John.

"Ready?" he asked, as Christine gripped Tyler.

"What about Mason?"

"That old daredevil?" John asked with a laugh. "He'll be fine!"

Then they were off, gliding at lightning speed down the snowy white slope.

"Whee!" Tyler shouted. "Whoohoo!"

Christine laughed with giddy delight, feeling like a child again herself.

"What do you think of Vermont?" John asked with a husky whisper.

The truth was that she loved it. Loved it even more than she could have imagined.

"It's perfect," she said with a happy sigh.

John hugged them a little tighter and settled his chin on her shoulder.

"I'm glad."

Chapter One

Christine sat at her drafting table and focused intently on her sketch. In the background, cheery Christmas music played from her high-end system. Dan had bought it three years before as a Christmas gift for her. Christine tightened her lips in concentration, ignoring the familiar ache in her heart. She couldn't quite get the angle of the sleigh. Perhaps if she brought it down closer to the rooftop...

"Mommy, it's almost—"

Christine startled at the tug on her sleeve, nearly upsetting her coffee. She gripped the mug to steady it. "Tyler! How many times have I told you not to—?"

Saucerlike eyes brimmed with tears. "But I'm late for school," he said, flagging his tyke-size cell in her direction. He clutched his big, black teddy bear, the one with the tattered ear. Christine's cheeks sagged as her baby boy stood before the snowy window. Flakes beat down harder outside, but work—and preschool—would go on. This was Chicago, after all.

She drew Tyler into her arms, awash with shame. How many times had she snapped at him this week already? And it was only Tuesday. "Mommy loves you very much," she said into his charcoal curls. "I'm so sorry."

"I love you, too, Mommy," his tiny, muffled voice returned.

Christine hugged him tighter, her gaze caught by a framed photo of Dan in his military fatigues standing with his new bride. He'd been so handsome and hopeful at the time. When Tyler smiled, he looked just like him.

Christine thought back to the happy, carefree brunette Dan had fallen in love with, wondering what he might think of her now. Her role as a single parent clearly didn't allow her to be carefree, but she wouldn't trade being a mother for the world. Dan had left her with a host of happy memories, but the best gift he'd supplied snuggled up against her here.

Ellen was right in urging them to get away. Apart from being Christine's boss at the greeting card company where she worked, Ellen was also her best friend. Ellen had noted the toll these last two years had taken on Christine and declared Christine was becoming ragged around the edges. Not only that, she was losing touch with her growing son. Christine denied it at first, but she could see it was true. A single tear slid down her cheek as she took in the Christmas decorations around them. Perhaps getting away would be good for her and Tyler, both.

"Mommy?" Tyler said.

"Yes, baby?"

"You're holding me so tight I can't breathe."

Christine released him and thumbed his nose.

"You really are the best little boy a mom could hope for. You know that?"

"And you're the best mom," he said with deeply sincere eyes.

Children can be so wonderfully forgiving, Christine thought with a tender sigh.

"It's snowing awfully hard out there," she said, her voice brightening.

Tyler raised his brow. "Yeah?"

"Yeah." Christine shot him an impish smile. "So, how's about you and me taking a little detour on our way into town?"

THE CHRISTMAS CATCH

John turned his attention on Tyler, waiting eagerly nearby.

"Ever been on a toboggan, young man?"

Tyler shook his head.

"Well then, you're in for a treat. Hop on!" he instructed, positioning Tyler right behind Mason. Tyler promptly wrapped his arms around the dog, who leaned back to lick his face.

"Will he be all right?" Christine asked with concern.

"Sure. You'll be right behind him, holding on."

"And where will you be?"

"I'll be hanging on to you." John grinned and her heart melted.

Christine warned herself not to get carried away. It was just an outing in the country. But when John settled in behind her and snuggled her and little Tyler securely in his arms, she couldn't help but blush in his embrace. He was so strong and capable. Though the steep slope ahead looked formidable, Christine had no qualms about her and Tyler heading down it with John.

"Ready?" he asked, as Christine gripped Tyler.

"What about Mason?"

"That old daredevil?" John asked with a laugh. "He'll be fine!"

Then they were off, gliding at lightning speed down the snowy white slope.

"Whee!" Tyler shouted. "Whoohoo!"

Christine laughed with giddy delight, feeling like a child again herself.

"What do you think of Vermont?" John asked with a husky whisper.

The truth was that she loved it. Loved it even more than she could have imagined.

"It's perfect," she said with a happy sigh.

John hugged them a little tighter and settled his chin on her shoulder.

"I'm glad."

Tyler bounced on his heels. "Oh boy! You mean...?"

"I don't think Auntie Ellen would fault me too much for running an hour behind on such a snowy day."

"Can I get the Happy Stack?"

Christine ruffled her fingers through his hair, her heart brimming with affection. "You, little man, may order anything that you want."

He beamed from ear to ear, a pint-size image of his dad.

"And while we're there," Christine continued. "I'll tell you all about our upcoming trip to Vermont."

Tyler scrunched up his face. "Vermont? What's that?"

"It's a state, sweetheart. Just a little ways away."

He paused, considering this, then held his teddy up to his ear. "Jasper wants to know if there'll be snow there."

"At least as much as we've got here."

Tyler listened to his teddy again. "Will we be there for Christmas?"

"You bet!"

Tyler hung his head, drawing Jasper into his chest.

Christine reached out a hand and gently raised his chin. "What's wrong, honey?"

Tyler glanced at his Christmas stocking, then swallowed hard.

"Jasper doesn't think Santa will be able to find us."

"Trust me on this," Christine said with a knowing air. "Santa will *always* be able to find us. Don't you know he has his magical ways?"

Tyler twisted his lips in thought. "You mean like a GPS?"

A chuckle escaped her, in spite of herself.

"Something like that," she said, steering Tyler toward the door. "Come on, let's grab our coats. The Pancake Palace awaits!"

Christine sat in Ellen's office in a glitzy skyscraper, a hazy view of the river just visible through the pounding snow.

"I'm glad you're taking me up on this," Ellen said, handing the plane tickets and a house key across her desk.

"It's not exactly like I had a choice," Christine said, accepting them.

Ellen shifted in her expensive leather chair. She was good at what she did and ran this department without a hitch. Christine only wished Ellen would give her a chance to prove herself as something more than a copywriter. Apart from having a knack for turning a phrase, Christine had artistic talent, too. She was certain she could put her own line together, given the opportunity. She'd fleshed out several concepts already, but Ellen wouldn't even take a look. Ellen said she was burning out, that she needed to get away and recharge her batteries. No sense branching off into something new when Christine could barely keep up with the day-to-day, as it was.

Ellen centered her snazzy red frames on her nose, then said with assurance, "You'll love it up there. Nice and peaceful, the perfect getaway for you and your boy. Give you two a chance to reconnect."

"Plus, I'm doing you a favor," Christine reminded her.

Ellen laughed heartily, tossing her chin-length auburn hair. "All right, already. You're doing me a favor."

Ellen's book editor cousin was vacationing in Europe and needed a house sitter. Ellen, who generally accepted the holiday task, was jetting down to Mexico with some hot new number. Christine admired Ellen's chutzpah in sticking with the dating scene year after year. Disappointments never seemed to faze her, and she remained hopeful—one boyfriend after the next—that this guy was finally the one.

"So, when do you go on vacation?" Christine asked.

"Day after tomorrow. Same day as you."

"Guess you'll be packing more lightly."

"If you're asking whether I'm taking the string bikini, the answer is yes."

Christine was impressed with her older friend. Ellen was fifty but still had the figure of a woman in her thirties. Of course, Ellen and her Stairmaster worked at it. Christine got her workouts chasing after Tyler.

"How old is this guy?" Christine asked, betting he was several years younger.

Ellen furiously fanned her face with some desk papers. "Of age," she said slyly. Suddenly, her face lit up. "Say! Maybe you'll meet someone in New England?"

Christine stood, gathering her things. "You're forgetting one very important fact. I'm not looking."

"Pays to keep your eyes open," Ellen said with a smile.

Chapter Two

"Mommy! Look out!" Tyler yelped from the backseat. Christine gripped the steering wheel of the huge SUV, wrenching them off to the side of the road and out of the path of the oncoming pickup. Her heart beat furiously as she brought the car to a halt and cursed the driving snow. This wasn't some idyllic New England snowfall; they were caught up in a blizzard, one as blinding as they come.

"Tyler, baby," she asked, reaching back and laying a hand on his leg. "Are you all right?"

She caught his big-eyed gaze in the rearview mirror. "That was cool! Can we do it again?"

"No," Christine answered, breathing heavily. "We most certainly can't do it again."

Just then something knocked at her driver's side window. Christine glanced quickly at Tyler, then cautiously lowered the glass.

A handsome man with a rugged face and stunning blue eyes peered into her vehicle.

"Everyone okay in there?" He wore a deep blue parka, jeans, and sturdy boots. A large golden retriever bounded up behind him, leaping against the side of the SUV and perching its paws on Christine's windowsill.

"Doggie!" Tyler cried happily.

"Well hey there, little fellow," the man said kindly before sternly commanding his dog. "Mason, get back in the truck."

The dog immediately obeyed, springing inside the truck that sat across the road with its driver's door ajar. The man turned his gaze on Christine and she unexpectedly felt her heart skip a beat. She judged him to be in his thirties, maybe five or six years older than she was.

"Yes, yes. We're fine."

"Good to hear," the man said. "You nearly ran me off the road back there."

"I nearly—?"

He shared a warming smile. "It's not that I mind. It's how it all comes out in the end that matters."

She stared at him dumbfounded, lost in his blue gaze. He probably thought she was some sort of inexperienced city slicker. And he was right. Christine didn't even own a car in Chicago and it had been some time since she'd driven one. She'd never been in anything with four-wheel drive, particularly anything this big.

"Where you folks headed?"

Christine lifted a map from the front console and handed it to him. The GPS had gotten them so lost, she'd turned if off over an hour ago. "Are we even going the right way?"

He studied the name of the village she'd circled, as the wind picked up around him. "Only if you want to take the long way there."

"Oh, no."

"You need to stay on this road for about five more miles then turn right at the fork. From there, you can follow the signs toward town. You got enough gas to help you along?"

Christine nodded, feeling her tension ease. Things would be all right, wouldn't they? It hadn't even been snowing when she'd picked up the SUV. Surely they were caught up in a sudden burst of storm that would abate in a short while.

The man stepped back and surveyed her vehicle with a shrill whistle.

"Looks like that front tire's wedged in pretty deep."

Her previous panic regained steam. "We're stuck here, aren't we?"

"Not for long," he said with a grin. "Lucky for you, I carry a chain in my truck."

Christine blinked hard, trying to gather her thoughts. She didn't even know this guy, but still, when he looked at her, her silly heart went all a-flutter. Ellen was right. She'd been out of the scene so long she'd lost her ability to cope. She apparently couldn't even make casual conversation with an attractive man without assessing his age and availability. Not that she was in the market, or anything like that. For all she knew, Mr. Good Samaritan and his trusty dog were taken. Though it was impossible to know about a wedding band, given the sensible gloves on his hands. Christine gasped when she realized that she'd been checking.

"Just hold it nice and steady!" he called through the howling winds. "I'm going to pull up ahead of you. Then, once you get going, I'll let the chain drop. Whatever you do, keep your eyes on the road—and don't stop!"

Christine's heart hammered against her chest as she gripped the wheel. How nutty could she be? She was here to rebuild things with Tyler, not to find some fly-by-night romance for herself. She didn't even believe in romance anymore. She'd already had the romance of a lifetime with Tyler's dad, and he'd left her with responsibilities. At the moment, her number one priority lay in getting her son to safety.

"Get ready now!" the man shouted. "On three! One… Two…"

"Mommy, I gotta pee," Tyler interjected.

"Not now, baby. Just hold it."

"Three!"

At once, the front of their vehicle was airborne and Christine feared they'd careen off the road. Then the pickup moved ahead at a gradual pace until her fishtailing SUV centered itself on the road. Sweat beaded her brow as Christine muttered prayers under her breath. Finally, they were moving forward, going straight as an arrow down the narrow road. The pickup slowed, pulling onto the shoulder to let her pass. The heavy chain dropped to the snowy lane. Christine glanced in her rearview mirror as the man scurried out of his truck to scoop it off the road, his tail-wagging dog behind him.

"Who was that?" Tyler asked, as the pickup faded from sight.

Christine heaved a grateful sigh. "Our guardian angel."

John sat in his truck with Mason, watching the beautiful woman and her son disappear through the snowdrifts. The kid was cute enough, but it was the mom who'd held his attention. What with those big, dark eyes and that long brown hair that fell in waves to her shoulders, it would be impossible for a man not to notice. Still, it was nonsensical that he'd paid attention to her looks. It wasn't like he'd consider dating someone that homicidal behind the wheel. Besides, where there was a boy, there was bound to be a father. John was nowhere near interested in getting tangled up in that. He had his fair share of picks in Burlington, and had always steered clear of single mothers. He wasn't even sure he had room for a woman in his life. At this point in his career, a full-blown family was a nonstarter. If she was still married to the boy's dad, that was even worse. John wouldn't be touching that with a twenty-foot pole.

John pushed back his parka hood and shook his head, attempting to clear it. Maybe the December air had gotten to him, because here he was, thinking all sorts of crazy thoughts about a woman he didn't even know. From the way she'd been totally thrown by the landscape and the tags on the rental SUV, she wasn't a local resident anyhow, just someone passing through. Chances of seeing her around were minimal. But what did that matter to him? The most important thing was that she and her son got to where they were going without running themselves—or anyone else—off the road again.

"What did you think, old boy?" he asked, patting the retriever's head.

The dog barked loudly.

"Yeah, they seemed like city slickers to me, too."

Christine pulled the SUV to the side of the road and double-checked the address. Just ahead of them sat a classic farmhouse nestled in a snowy field behind a split-rail fence. She stepped into the biting cold to wipe the snow off of the sign dangling from a post at the head of the drive. WINTERHAVEN appeared in stenciled lettering. Winds whipped up as Christine battled her way back to the SUV, shielding her face with her coat sleeve. She clambered into the driver's seat with a shiver and cranked up the heat another notch.

"Looks like we're home," she said softly to Tyler, who snoozed in his car seat. They'd paused for a potty break ten miles earlier then he'd promptly passed out from exhaustion. Not even the chill of the wind on his face woke him up as she carried him toward the house.

Moments later, Christine carted her sleeping boy over the threshold of the old-style structure. The great room was cozy yet elegant, with exposed wood beams and a large stone hearth. A fire had been laid for them in advance, a neat stack of logs and extra kindling sticks piled in a box nearby.

"Nice," Christine said to herself.

She decided to let Tyler rest on the sofa while she settled in. After laying him down and covering him with a handy throw blanket, she perused the rest of the place. The kitchen was expansive and well equipped, and the three bedrooms upstairs were every bit as comfortable, with four-poster beds and huge down comforters. From each window, visions of a winter wonderland beckoned her to run outside and play. Christine felt her inner child delight in the thought of making snowmen and snow angels, then racing indoors to hot cocoa and homemade cookies. Maybe Ellen was more right about this trip than she knew. A fresh change in scenery and limited interruptions could set just the right stage for quality Mommy and Tyler time.

A little while later, Christine sat at the large farm table near the front of the great room sipping her coffee and studying directions to the local market. Tyler stirred, then sat up and rubbed his eyes, yawning.

"Where are we?" he asked, clutching Jasper.

"Winterhaven."

"Huh?"

"It's where we're staying, baby. What do you think?"

He looked around, still a little dazed.

"Where's the TV?"

"I don't think there is one."

His small lips pulled into a pout.

"What's there to do?"

"Plenty! There are puzzles over there in the cupboard. Legos, Lincoln Logs…"

"Lincoln who?" he asked, astounded.

"I'll show you, honey. It's fun."

Unconvinced, Tyler scooped his little backpack off the floor and extracted a portable video game. Next, he dug out its charger, settling back on the sofa to survey the surrounding lamps. "Least there's 'lectricity."

Christine studied her son, thinking he was a tad too modern for his own good. She had to admit, though, that even she'd forgotten about old-fashioned fun stuff like roasting marshmallows until she'd walked in here. "You hungry?" she queried, thinking he must be.

Dark eyes lit up. "Deep-dish Chicago pizza?"

"Not here."

"Oh," he said, disappointed.

Christine folded the map in her hands, noting the snow had stopped outside. It was likely a temporarily lull in the weather. Best to take advantage while they could.

"I was just reading about the local market. I'm not sure if they'll have pizza, but they're bound to have provisions. How about you and I head over there and check it out?"

Chapter Three

Christine halted her brimming shopping cart in the aisle as Tyler dropped in a huge bag of marshmallows. They were at Mac's Market, the sole grocers in the tiny village on the outskirts of Burlington. Already they had chocolate bars and graham crackers. Their list was nearly complete. "Can't forget the cocoa," she said, smiling at her son. She reached for it but it was high on a shelf, all the way to the back.

"Here, let me help with that," a familiar masculine voice said over her shoulder.

Christine heard a happy bark and turned to find the man from the road behind her. He wore winter boots, jeans, and a gray college sweatshirt beneath his open parka. Up close and personal, he looked even better than he had outdoors, his short dark hair and ruddy complexion a heady complement to his eyes.

"Well, hello," he said with a smile. Mason wriggled on his haunches beside him, wagging his tail. Tyler stared up at the guy and his jaw dropped.

"Are you really an angel?"

"Beg pardon?"

"Mommy says you're an angel."

Christine felt her face flush. "Oh no, I think he misunderstood. I was just… What I mean is…" She glanced down at Mason, then up at him, amazed. "They let dogs in here?"

The man leaned forward with a confidential whisper. "He doesn't know he's a dog. He thinks he's a college student."

Why did the mention of college spark some vague recognition? Christine's eyes locked on his sweatshirt. "Carolina?" she asked with surprise.

"The University of North Carolina at Chapel Hill," he said with pride.

"No way."

"Way."

"You went there?"

"Most certainly did."

"Small world."

"And you?"

She looked at him and smiled. "I know why the sky's Carolina blue."

"God's a Tar Heel," he said with a laugh.

Tyler studied him with awe. "I thought you might know God."

The man eyed Tyler curiously. "Here," he said to Christine, "let me help you with that cocoa." He reached for it and easily took it from the shelf, handing it to her. She accepted it, inexplicably spellbound as his blue eyes crinkled at the corners.

"You know, I never got the chance to thank you for our daring rescue."

"Oh, it wasn't so daring," he said.

"We could have been stuck there for hours."

"How's the SUV holding up?"

"As long as I stay on the road it works like a charm."

They shared a bout of companionable laughter, then stood there staring at each other as if each wanted to speak but neither could think up anything to say.

"Well, I guess that's it, then," Christine offered awkwardly. "We'd best finish up. It's been a long day."

"Of course."

John thoughtfully watched them walk away, feeling an unfamiliar tug in his chest. She was just some girl from Carolina. So what if she'd wound up in Vermont? That didn't mean she'd be interested, and certainly didn't indicate she was available. Mason stood beside him, itching to follow after the woman and her son. How come his dog always knew things he didn't?

"You know I was thinking," John called out.

She turned on her heels, her cheeks flushed.

"I was just thinking the same thing."

"You were?"

"I mean, I meant to tell you... wanted to say, it was really great running into you."

Boy, was she a looker with those big, dark eyes and neatly compact figure. She was even prettier than he'd given her credit for in the SUV.

"Yeah, you too. But, you know, I was wondering…" Mason interjected a happy bark, not wanting to be left out. "My dog and I were wondering… what's a Carolina girl like you doing all the way up here?"

"I'm a Chicago girl now," she said, taking her son's hand.

"The question stands."

"We're house-sitting for a friend," she said with a sweet smile. "And you?"

John shifted on his feet, feeling as if she were assessing him. He'd probably forgotten to shave or something. "I teach over at the college." He mentally kicked himself for the one little detail that had slipped his mind. "My apologies," he said extending his hand. "I never introduced myself. I'm John Steadman."

She stepped forward to accept his grip and John caught a whiff of her perfume. She smelled all sweet and womanly, like a field full of wildflowers in summertime.

"Christine White. Nice to meet you."

Soulful dark eyes met his and John felt the back of his neck flash hot. There was a tug at his sleeve and John looked down.

"I'm Tyler!" the little boy said, bouncing on his heels.

John kneeled to greet him at eye level, man to man.

"Good to know ya, little fellow," he said, firmly shaking Tyler's hand. "You taking good care of your mom?"

Tyler nodded solemnly and John chuckled.

"Well, keep up the good work!"

Mason held up a paw in Tyler's direction. John glanced at Christine for her approval, got it, then looked at the boy. "Seems like Mason wants to shake hands, too."

Ten minutes later, they stood in the snow outside the rental SUV where John had helped load groceries in the back. While it had been fun running into them, John didn't have the nerve to suggest seeing them again. What kind of sense would that make? Christine and Tyler were bound to have made their own vacation plans, and John had plenty to take care of too.

"You and Tyler take care, Christine," John said, waving good-bye.

"Thanks, you too," she said through her open window. Tyler raised a mitten and called good-bye to the dog as they backed out and slowly pulled away.

John watched their taillights fade as Mason stood by with a sullen expression.

"Don't look so down, fellow," John told him, stroking his head. "Santa's coming soon."

The dog gave him a sideways glance like he'd just made the biggest mistake of his life. Okay, so maybe he'd noticed she wasn't wearing a wedding ring, but that didn't mean he had to act on it.

"And none of that nonsense about how I should have gotten her number," John scolded, adjusting his parka. "I have a very occupied life."

But Mason just ignored him and loped through the snow toward their truck.

Chapter Four

Christine whisked about the kitchen, talking on her cell while she fixed dinner. A pot of chili simmered on the stove as she mixed a cornbread batter. The snow had started up again outside, beating down harder than ever, but they were snug inside their getaway. "Hang on, Ellen," she said into the receiver. "Just let me check on Ty a sec." She peered through the swinging door to find him happily engaged in a game of Legos by the fire.

"So?" Ellen asked as Christine popped the cornbread pan in the oven. "Is it as lovely as I said?"

"Just beautiful," Christine answered, gazing out the window. "And very, very cold."

"I wish I could sympathize…" Christine heard a low murmuring in the background. It was Ellen's voice, soft and sultry. "A little more on the shoulders, honey?"

"I'm sorry. I didn't get that."

"I was just saying I'm enjoying the warmth down here." She giggled and Christine could have sworn she heard the tinkling of a tropical drink in her hand. She even bet it held a little paper umbrella. She could just see Ellen in that tiny bikini wearing a big straw hat and gigantic dark glasses. "Cancun's been incredibly welcoming."

The man Ellen was with was bound to be scorching hot. It wasn't like Christine hadn't met her own share of hunks, as well. "I know what you mean," she said in a mysterious tone. "Vermont's been friendly, too."

There was a subtle slurping, then a startled cough. "Don't tell me the confirmed bachelorette has met someone?"

"I didn't say that... exactly."

"You've been there all of eight hours! Good girl!" Christine could tell Ellen was pleased with her, probably beaming like the Cheshire cat from ear to ear.

"It's not like that at all. My SUV got stuck in a snowstorm."

"And Prince Charming rescued you? Ooh, I'm just loving it! Come now, dish to the woman who made it all possible. What's his name?"

"John Steadman."

"Sounds promising. What's he do?"

"He's a college professor."

"I'll Google him!" Then Christine heard her whisper to her boy toy. "Hand me my iPad, baby."

"That's stalkerish!"

"You're just jealous because you didn't do it first. Let's see S... T... Is it just an 'e' or an 'ea' in Steadman?"

"How should I know?"

"Yep. It's 'ea.' Here he is. Mister... Whoops! Make that *Doctor* John Steadman. Um-hum... Burlington, Vermont. My oh my oh my. Is he a hottie!

"Ellen!"

"What? I'm terribly proud of you. *So,* when are the two of you going out?"

"That's what I've been trying to tell you. We're not."

"Why not?"

"He didn't ask."

"Then you ask him."

"We're only here for two weeks."

"And I'm only here for one," she purred. "That doesn't mean I'm letting *my* vacation go to waste." Christine feared she heard kissing and hoped Ellen wasn't making out on the other end of the line.

"I'm not like you, Ellen. This is different. I'm—"

"Chicken."

"No. Out of practice."

"That's the whole point, Christine. It's been over two years. Don't you think it's time?"

Christine opened her laptop and set it on the counter. Of all the nerve! Ellen went and Googled her guy before she'd had a chance to. Christine felt a rash of embarrassment for thinking of John Steadman as hers. She hadn't laid claim to him, for heaven's sake. They barely even knew each other and had only met a couple of times. By accident. Literally.

Suddenly a smoke alarm sounded and Christine looked up to find chili bubbling over on the cooktop and black smoke curling from the oven. "Oh no!" she cried, leaping from the barstool.

Tyler rushed into the room, hollering, "Something's on fire!"

She grabbed two potholders and pulled the charred cornbread from the oven. Quickly opening the kitchen door, she tossed the seared pan out in the snow, then dashed back inside to wave a towel beneath the blaring smoke detector.

Tyler clambered up on the kitchen stool to watch the show as the air cleared and the wailing instrument finally quieted.

"Whew!" Christine breathed, dabbing her forehead with the dishtowel.

Tyler slowly spun his stool toward the counter, then cried with delight.

"Mommy, Mommy! Look! It's our angel!"

Christine crossed to the counter and shut her laptop.

"John's not an angel, baby. I already explained that to you."

"But, when he helped us you said—"

"It was a figure of speech. Something someone says when they mean something else."

"But that doesn't make any sense."

"That's how people talk sometimes."

"Why don't they just say what they mean?"

"I guess that would be too easy." She reached for her son and helped him off of the stool. "Come on, let's get ready to eat. You hungry for dinner?"

Tyler wrinkled his nose. "Can I skip the cornbread?"

An hour later, Christine and Tyler were constructing a fortress out of Lincoln Logs. Tyler crowned the final turret with a tiny toy flag. "Tadahh!" he proclaimed proudly. "It's done!"

Christine's heart swelled with pride. She was so honored to call this charming young man her son. "It's awesome, Ty. World's best."

Tyler beamed.

"You see," Christine told him, "playing the old-fashioned way isn't really so rotten."

"It's all right, I guess." Tyler yawned and rubbed his eyes.

Christine checked the mantel clock, seeing it was after nine.

"Oh gosh, look at the time. It's up to bed with you."

"But mom—" he protested, even as he picked up Jasper.

"No buts about it. There will be more time for play tomorrow."

"You mean it?"

Christine nodded as he headed up the stairs dragging his teddy beside him. Slowly, thoughtfully, he turned toward his mom. "I like Vermont," he said.

"Yeah, buddy," she answered, smiling softly, "I like it, too."

Chapter Five

With Tyler tucked in, Christine sat at the dining room table to work on her drafts. Her first task was reworking her earlier sketch of Santa's sleigh over a rooftop by using Winterhaven as a model for the scene. After a while, tired from her labors, she stood for a stretch and walked to the window, surveying the already buried-in-snow SUV. *Guardian Angel,* she thought with a chuckle, casting her gaze up the stairs to where Tyler lay sleeping.

Nabbing her laptop off of an end table, she carried it with her to the sofa and perched it on her knees. Within seconds, a computerized voice told her she had mail. Curious, Christine opened her messages to find a new e-mail in her inbox from, of all things, the University of North Carolina Alumni Association. She thought of John, but then realized she was being ridiculous to take this sheer coincidence as any sort of sign. Even if they had gone to the same school, she reasoned, they probably hadn't been there at the same time. He had to be in his mid to late thirties at least, and she had just turned thirty-one. Still, she couldn't keep herself from clicking over to his Web page, which she'd bookmarked earlier, to review its details one more time.

Department Chair John Steadman is a full professor of business and economics. Steadman holds a BA from the University of North Carolina at Chapel Hill and a PhD from the Massachusetts Institute of Technology. Before coming to Vermont, Professor Steadman served an associate and then full professor at

Tulane University in New Orleans, where he was instrumental in developing innovative business models.

Below his bio and an extremely flattering professional photo, a link directed the reader to *Contact Professor Steadman.* Christine could just bet that a number of coeds had the hots for the steamy professor. Lots of girls got crushes on their teachers, and John's easygoing nature and gentle charm would make him easy to fall for. His ruggedly handsome face and that built, athletic body didn't hurt much either... But Christine was no college kid. She was a full-grown woman and a mother besides. She was way too mature to go crushing on people, particularly people she didn't know that well.

Christine pondered the prospect of getting to know John. Perhaps Ellen was right. Christine hadn't gone out for so much as coffee with a man since Dan died. She couldn't sequester herself forever. What was the harm in a casual connection anyway? Maybe being in Vermont for a limited time made it all the better, less risky somehow. She could take a chance on seeing someone on a friendship basis, where circumstance clearly dictated that a friendship was all it could be. She wasn't ready for full-scale dating. Plus, she had Tyler to consider. Though he was too young to remember a lot about his dad, he'd already lost a father once. Christine didn't want to put him in the position of forming an attachment that might not pan out. Truth be told, she didn't want to put herself in that situation either.

And yet, *getting back out there,* as Ellen called it, didn't have to be such a scary proposition. Christine could take it in little, bitty, baby steps. That's right, one thing at a time. This Christmas, maybe she'd brave a coffee date in Vermont. Next year, who knew? She might work her way up to lunch with someone. By the time Tyler was eighteen, she might even find herself ready for sleepovers… A flash of heat tore through her as she suddenly imagined herself going to bed with John. But that was a ridiculous thing to consider. Plain crazy. She wasn't interested in anything like that right now. She'd already thought the whole thing through.

Christine gingerly guided the mouse over the e-mail link, wondering if she could really do it. She'd been raised so traditionally that she didn't totally feel comfortable making the first move. Then again, if it was a simple move toward friendship, what was the big deal? A vision of John sweeping her into his arms raced through her mind, and she slapped her laptop shut, losing her nerve. She stood and skittishly began to pace the room. "On the one hand," she said out loud. "It's no harm, no foul. I just write and say, thanks again. That's innocent enough. I don't have to be the one to suggest going out. I'll leave that to him. And, well… if he doesn't, there's nothing lost."

Feeling her courage surge, Christine sat on the sofa again and reopened her laptop. She slapped it shut two seconds later. "On the other hand, what does that say? That I can't get him off my mind? He'd clearly know I looked him up! What kind of woman does that? A desperate one, obviously..."

She set her laptop on a sofa cushion and strode to the bar, thinking some merlot might help. Either to grant her the wherewithal to go through with it, or realize what a cockeyed idea it was. She poured herself a glass, still musing aloud. "Then again, I am a fellow Tar Heel, and we Carolina types are always friendly with each other." She took a long swallow, draining her glass. She was worse off than she thought. Talking to herself and swigging down wine! Something had to be done, and fast!

Christine sat back down with fire in her belly and determination in her soul. If Ellen could do this, then so could she, damn it. It wasn't like she was proposing marriage. She was only writing to establish contact. She clicked the link and a dialogue box opened. Now, if she could just think of the perfect thing to say.

John opened his e-mail the next morning and was pleased to find a message from Christine White. "Who says it's not an equal opportunity world?" he asked Mason, who was scarfing down his breakfast. "Hey," he said to the dog, who just kept eating. "Hey!"

Mason stopped chomping and looked up.

"Yeah, I'm talking to you," John said with a grin. "Guess what, buddy? I think we've got a date."

Mason cocked his head sideways, waiting.

"No, I haven't asked her yet. But that doesn't mean I'm not going to."

John took a sip of his coffee, devising a plan. The truth was that he was inordinately happy to hear from Christine. She hadn't said much, just *Thanks again for the 'absolutely daring' rescue* or some such, but it was what was written between the lines that counted. She'd looked him up! Had actually taken the time to track him down, despite the fact that she couldn't be in town for more than just a few days. John reasoned there wasn't much harm in taking her and her boy out for coffee and cocoa. Show them a bit of genuine New England hospitality. Heck, it was lonely up here in wintertime. Besides, maybe his best friend Carlos was right. Spending all his time trapped indoors with a dog was getting to him. Sooner or later, he was going to start hearing Mason talk back.

It wasn't like John didn't have his lady friends. But honestly, none of them were as good as Mason to talk to. It happened every time. Just when John thought things were going really well, someone had to bring up the marriage talk, that someone not being him. It wasn't that John was opposed to marriage in theory. It was extra good for the economy, in fact. Just not for him personally at the moment, not with his big promotion coming up and his professional papers due. Maybe one day he'd settle down, but it didn't need to be any day soon. Fortunately, that was neither here nor there. That sweet Carolina girl was only here for a little while, so there was no harm in being friendly and making a connection. All in the spirit of the General Alumni Association of course, John thought, beginning to type.

Christine sat up in bed and flipped open her laptop. Yes. There was a message from John Steadman! *Coffee and cocoa this afternoon? I know a place that you and Tyler might enjoy.*

Christine grinned broadly and quickly typed back *Yes*.

"Yes, yes, *yes!*" she hollered, merrily kicking her feet under the covers. He'd done it. The handsome professor hottie had actually gone and done it! Asked Christine and Tyler out on a date! Okay, so maybe it wasn't a date, technically. An outing then, yes. That's what it was, an outing. Just the three of them. Four, counting Mason. She was sure that he would come along. Tyler was bound to love that. *"Yes!"*

Christine brought her hands to her flaming cheeks as Tyler pressed his way in the room. "Mommy?" he asked groggily. "What is it? Is it time to get up?"

"I'm sorry if I woke you, honey. I was just making plans. How does having cocoa with John sound?"

He looked at her uncertainly. "It sounds all right."

Christine deposited her computer on the floor. "Come here, you," she said, giving her little boy and his teddy a hug. She was still grinning in spite of herself, as gleeful and nervous as a teenager.

Tyler peered up at her with big, dark eyes. "Are you happy, Mommy?"

She pulled him up onto the bed and nestled him firmly in her arms. "Yeah, I suppose I am."

"I like it when you're happy," he said, snuggling up against her. "You're not like that much."

The simple declaration hit her like a sucker punch. "Oh baby, I'm so sorry," she said, hearing her voice crack. "Sorry that Mommy's been such a crank."

"It's not your fault," his little voice said.

"What do you mean?"

"I know you need friends too."

She jostled him in her arms.

"I've got Auntie Ellen."

"That's not enough."

"No?"

"Billy's mommy has a friend."

"Oh?"

"Sometimes he sleeps over."

Christine swallowed hard. "We don't need to worry about that."

"I wouldn't mind."

"But Mommy would. She's... I'm... not ready."

"Well, I think John's nice. Even if he's not an angel."

"I bet you like Mason too," she said, kissing him on the head.

Tyler grinned. "I like Mason best!"

Chapter Six

Christine, Tyler, and John sat in the small café housed in a country cottage. A real wood fire blazed in the fireplace nearby, its mantel crowned with Christmas decorations. A sign on the opposite wall read *Kiddy Korner*. Below it children played with old style blocks, puzzles, and a handcrafted circus train, stocked with various animals. Tyler set down his hot chocolate and pointed across the room.

"Can I go over there?"

Christine dabbed his upper lip with a napkin. "Sure baby, go right ahead." She turned to John. "This place is great."

He grinned at her, blue eyes crinkling. "I thought you and Tyler might like it." At his feet, Mason lazily lifted his head. John patted him lightly and he went back to sleep.

"You're pretty good with kids," Christine told him. "Got any of your own?"

"Me? Oh no. I mean, not yet. Never married. I've got two nieces and a nephew, though."

"Are they close by?"

"I wish, but no. They're with their mom in Baltimore. That's where I grew up."

He shifted awkwardly. "And you and Tyler? Are you all on your own in Chicago? Any family there?"

"It's just the two of us," she said. "My husband, Dan, Tyler's dad, passed away a few years ago."

"I'm sorry, Christine. I had no—"

"It's all right. It's good for me to talk about it."

"Was it an illness?" he asked tentatively.

"Afghanistan."

John was quiet a moment. When he spoke his voice was tinged with compassion. "Things must be hard, getting by on your own with a young son."

"Ty and I manage," she said, sounding braver than she felt. The truth was that she hadn't been managing well at all lately.

"You seem to do a great job..." His lips creased in a subtle smile. "...except for when you're driving in snowstorms."

"Hey!" she cried in mock offense, but secretly she appreciated his effort to lighten the moment. Mason awakened, startled by her shout of surprise. John slipped him biscotti under the table to quell his interest. The dog took it and gnawed contentedly.

"So tell me," John said, changing the subject. "What do you do in Chicago?"

"I'm a copywriter for a major greeting card company."

"That sounds interesting."

"Not as interesting as I'd like."

"What do you mean?"

"I basically write the words, but it's always been my dream to illustrate too. You know, develop my own line—soup to nuts."

"Why not go for it?"

"It's not as easy as all that," she said with a frown. "Company politics."

"So? Start your own company."

"What?"

"What's stopping you?" John leaned forward with his challenge.

Christine sat back. "Oh, about a million things. First, I'd have to raise the capital, find investors. I couldn't front even a small operation like that on my own. Then, I'd need to locate a printer, contract distributors…"

"None of that sounds impossible."

"Impossible, no. It's just nothing I've ever considered."

"With the Internet these days, there are bound to be new opportunities."

"Sure."

John took a slow sip of coffee, surveying her over the rim of his cup. After a beat, he surprised her by raising his cup to hers. "The future is long," he said with an enigmatic smile.

"Yes. Yes, it is," she answered thoughtfully. "Very long indeed."

She returned his toast, mulling over his proposition. *I mean, it would be a really big dream. Totally cool,* she thought. Just no way could it happen now. Maybe someday, when things were more settled…

Their eyes locked for a moment and Christine's cheeks flamed. All John had to do was look at her and old embers leapt into brushfires, igniting sensations all over her body. Christine hadn't felt those smoldering sensations in quite a while. In fact, she hadn't been sure they still existed. But they did and here they were, raging out of control. So much so that Christine nabbed some ice from her water glass and dumped it in her coffee. Drinking something hot at the moment seemed positively contrary when Christine clearly needed to cool down.

John swallowed hard and followed suit, likewise chilling his java. "It *is* a little warm in here," he said, his face coloring as well. She couldn't tell if it was from the warmth of the fire or from the way that she'd looked at him. In any case, his chiseled face was exceptionally handsome in the subtle glow.

He studied their water glasses, then stumbled slightly with the words. "In present day, we seem to be all out of ice. Should I get us some more?"

"That would be great, thanks."

When John returned, the conversation turned to something thankfully less personal, the topics of courses he taught at the business school. While Christine wasn't familiar with all the nuances, it was refreshing to talk to someone so enthusiastic about his work. Before she knew it, two hours had flown by and they were standing at the door ready to make their departure. Christine had nearly forgotten how good it felt to talk comfortably with a man. Maybe there'd been a few peaks and valleys during their dialogue, but overall they'd gotten on reasonably well. So well, in fact, that she couldn't help but feel slightly depressed that the outing was over.

"Come on, Ty," she told her son as he said good-bye to his newfound friends. "Let's get on your hat and gloves. It's awfully cold outside." Mason watched them with ears drooping, not wanting them to go.

"I'm really glad that you could make it," John said, helping Christine on with her coat.

"Thanks for asking us," she said, holding his gaze.

Just then, a middle-aged man barreled through the door carrying a blast of frigid air with him. Mason excitedly bounded for him, covering him with doggie kisses.

"Mason, down!" John said. This time Christine was sure he'd flushed red, from his neck to the tips of his ears. The dog slunk to the floor, looking embarrassed.

"Don't be so hard on the pooch," the man said. "Some days it's the only loving I get!" He unwrapped his broad scarf, exposing a handsome older face and a graying beard. He shot John a merry grin.

"Steadman! How's it going? Surviving sabbatical?"

John affectionately pumped his hand. "Good to see you, Carlos."

Carlos sent a quick glance at Tyler then gave Christine an appreciative once-over.

"Hello…" he said to Christine, his voice lilting with a light Spanish accent. "And you must be?"

"Christine White," she said, extending her hand.

"Carlos Dominguez. It's a pleasure." He turned his gaze on Ty. "And you, young man?"

John smiled. "This is Christine's son, Tyler."

Carlos eyed them all, apparently pleased with the situation.

"Well, well… Isn't this delightful? Where are you two from?"

"We're here from Chicago," Christine said.

"It's a permanent move, I hope?"

"Just a vacation," she told him.

"I didn't think my colleague had that much luck."

"Weren't you on your way somewhere?" John asked Carlos, clearly trying to get rid of him.

"Fine, fine," Carlos said, shaking his head. "I can see when I'm not wanted." He smiled warmly at Christine before taking his leave. "Christine, hope to have the opportunity again."

"I'll bet you do, you old dog," John said under his breath. Mason nuzzled his hand, but John waved him away.

"He seemed nice," Christine said as Carlos made his way to the coffee bar and ordered.

"We've been friends for a long time. Knew him down in New Orleans, in fact."

"At Tulane?" Christine queried before she could stop herself.

John dissected her with piercing blue eyes and her cheeks caught fire. Now he'd know she'd been stalking him. Not only had she looked up his e-mail address, she'd practically memorized his bio!

John cocked his head sideways and studied her with amazement. "That's right."

Christine slid on her gloves, anxious to extract herself from the humiliating moment. "Tyler and I should head back."

"That's not a bad thought," John said, peering out the door beside them. "It's starting to flurry out there."

"Does it ever stop snowing in Vermont?" Christine asked with a laugh.

"A few months out of the year," he answered.

Christine finished bundling up Tyler and pulled on her winter hat.

"You know," John said. "The snow may be a pain for driving, but it makes for awfully good sledding."

"Sledding? Yahoo!" Tyler crowed, springing up and down.

Christine stared at John, her heart hopeful. Oh to be in a winter wonderland with this handsome man, gliding down snow-covered hills. Christine brought her hand to her mouth, hoping she'd just thought that, not said it. By the way John's eyes crinkled at the corners, she wasn't sure.

"I was thinking," he said as a smile spread across his lips, "that maybe the three of us could go for a ride?"

"He knows where all the best hills are!" Carlos shouted from across the room.

Christine turned, to spy Carlos seated in the corner, apparently eavesdropping from behind his splayed newspaper.

John spouted back, feigning irritation. "Could you mind your own business for one fraction of a second… please?"

Carlos shrugged and rattled his paper, making Christine giggle out loud. Tyler stared up at her with joy in his eyes. "Can we Mommy? *Puhleeze?*"

John met her gaze and said firmly, "I do know where all the best hills are."

"Sledding sounds great," Christine said with a happy grin. "Only I don't think there's a sled at the house."

"No worries. I'll supply one. Where are you staying?"

"Winterhaven. Do you know it?"

"Know it?" John lowered his voice. "Carlos used to date the woman who lives there."

"Oh," Christine whispered back, intrigued. "What happened?"

"She's a very nice person," John replied quietly. "Just didn't share Carlos's sense of… adventure."

Christine's cell rang, startling her out of the moment.

"I'm sorry," she told John. She checked and saw the call was from Ellen. "I think I'd better take this."

"I hope you're having half as much fun as I am," Ellen chirped. Her voice wavered, almost as if it were windblown. "I'm about to go airborne!"

"What?" Christine shrieked, before getting herself under control and turning politely away from John and the other interested coffee patrons. She found herself facing Carlos, who pointedly lowered his paper. "Ellen, what on earth is going on?"

"Parasailing, Christine. My gorgeous man Emilio and I are setting our sights for the sun!"

"Be careful. That sounds dangerous."

"Dangerous, ha! It's a blast! This is our second time up!"

"Well, seeing as how you survived the first time, do you think I could call you back? I'm kind of busy with something."

"Just as long at that *something* spells his name S… T… E… A…"

Christine pressed End Call and whirled on her heels, finding herself nearly in John's arms. She backed away from his broad chest seconds before crashing into it.

"Everything all right?" he asked, steadying her by the elbows. Even through her layers of winter clothing, the electricity from his touch tore up her arms and sent tiny shivers racing down her spine. Christine's stomach flip-flopped. She wondered if she was getting sick or was just nervous. John's stare dove into her and she felt faint from his perusal. Had to be the nerves. Yeah, those combined with the coffee.

"Oh yes. Everything's fine." She affected a laugh. "That was just my best friend Ellen. Senior editor, too, but we're friends as well. Anyhow…" She drew a deep breath. "What time were you thinking about for sledding?"

He released her with a heartwarming grin. "How's two o'clock tomorrow sound?"

"Two o'clock sounds good." She smiled feebly in return, wondering if she looked as smitten as she suddenly felt. Oh God, was she crushing on the professor just like some silly coed? And right in front of the entire town's tiny population, including his inquisitive best friend?

Christine took Tyler's hand and raced out into the weather, hoping the frigid wind would drive some sense into her. She was only here on vacation, not poised to spend the rest of her life! What was she doing letting her emotions get the best of her?

"See you tomorrow!" she called, as she and Tyler headed for the SUV. "And thanks again!"

"Mommy?" Tyler asked as she snapped him into his car seat. "Is John your friend now?"

She smiled at him and answered uncertainly. "I think so, sweetie."

"It's about time!" he declared.

Chapter Seven

John couldn't believe he was doing this, taking Christine and her young son sledding. If he didn't know better, he'd swear he'd already tumbled headlong down a hill and taken a knock on the noggin. John wasn't even interested in getting involved. With that potential promotion looming, he had to make work his priority. When John made Associate Dean, *then* he could entertain thoughts of a personal life. Even if his advancement came off, he'd want to keep things clean and simple while he took to his new task. What he'd been doing up until now worked fine. Occasional outings with certain lady friends, no fuss and no strings attached. That was what he wanted, wasn't it?

John recalled that moment in the café when he'd been trapped in the heat of Christine's gaze. Hell, it had been more than one moment. There were several times, in fact, when he'd felt his pulse pounding and his reason racing into overdrive. It wasn't just that she was pretty; there was something else about her too. She was obviously smart and could hold her own in a conversation. And when she'd nearly landed in his arms, it was all John could do not to imagine bringing his mouth to hers. Seriously, it wasn't like she'd been graced with those lips for no reason. Clearly that reason had to do with her needing a good kissing now and again.

John strode toward his truck and deposited the handcrafted toboggan in its bed, determined to put these cockamamie notions out his head. The heavy snow had abated to a light sprinkle. It was the perfect afternoon for the occasion. What was so wrong with a toboggan ride anyhow? It wasn't exactly romantic, with the little boy coming along. It was more like a family outing. John swallowed hard at that last thought, feeling like he'd bitten off more than he could chew. Was it really so wrong to take them out, knowing they'd be gone in just a little while? Perhaps that was John's best form of protection. It was likely Christine's too. Surely she wouldn't want to become entangled with someone living so far away. Her life was complicated enough as it was. Mason barked and John looked down to see him furiously wagging his tail, apparently ready to get on with it. At least *he* wasn't conflicted.

John's cell rang and he tucked a hand inside his coat to pull it out.

"Your timing's rotten," he told Carlos.

"No, what's rotten is your holding out on me. Ten years together and you didn't breathe a word!"

"That's because there's nothing to talk about."

"Aha! I knew it. This one's really gotten to you, hasn't she?"

"Nobody gets to me, Carlos. You know that."

Carlos chuckled. "Not until now, amigo. Not until now. Not that I disapprove. Christine seems different somehow. Not quite so… eager."

"Please."

"You know what I mean. With the others, I could practically hear those talons springing out to catch you."

"You, my friend, have an overblown sense of the dramatic."

"I, compadre, have a total connection to the truth."

John opened the door of his truck and Mason sprang inside. "I'd love to chat all day," he said. "But the truth is I've got someplace to be."

"You're seeing her, aren't you? Probably her and that cute kid too."

John stared at Mason and shook his head before replying in a singsongy voice. "Good-bye, Carlos!"

Snow fell lightly as John lifted the toboggan from his truck. They were on a scenic hill, the splendor of the snowcapped countryside around them. Christine ran a gloved hand down the side of the toboggan, admiring the sheen of its wood.

"She's a beauty," she said to John. "Almost like a work of art."

He gave her a smile that swept the chill from the bitter wind. "Thanks. I appreciate that."

"Hang on…" she said with surprise. "Are you saying you made this?"

"Some time ago. It was one of my first pieces."

Christine was impressed. She'd never met a man who'd made a toboggan—or much of anything else—before. "You've made others?"

John positioned the toboggan on the hilltop and looked up. Mason immediately jumped on. "Toboggans, no," he said. "I figured one was all I needed. But I've built other things: bookshelves, tables, and the like."

"Tables? Really?"

"My dining room table in fact." He studied her thoughtfully. "I'll have to show it to you sometime."

Christine's cheeks warmed as she dropped her eyes. "I'd like that."

John turned his attention on Tyler, waiting eagerly nearby.

"Ever been on a toboggan, young man?"

Tyler shook his head.

"Well then, you're in for a treat. Hop on!" he instructed, positioning Tyler right behind Mason. Tyler promptly wrapped his arms around the dog, who leaned back to lick his face.

"Will he be all right?" Christine asked with concern.

"Sure. You'll be right behind him, holding on."

"And where will you be?"

"I'll be hanging on to you." John grinned and her heart melted.

Christine warned herself not to get carried away. It was just an outing in the country. But when John settled in behind her and snuggled her and little Tyler securely in his arms, she couldn't help but blush in his embrace. He was so strong and capable. Though the steep slope ahead looked formidable, Christine had no qualms about her and Tyler heading down it with John.

"Ready?" he asked, as Christine gripped Tyler.

"What about Mason?"

"That old daredevil?" John asked with a laugh. "He'll be fine!"

Then they were off, gliding at lightning speed down the snowy white slope.

"Whee!" Tyler shouted. "Whoohoo!"

Christine laughed with giddy delight, feeling like a child again herself.

"What do you think of Vermont?" John asked with a husky whisper.

The truth was that she loved it. Loved it even more than she could have imagined.

"It's perfect," she said with a happy sigh.
John hugged them a little tighter and settled his chin on her shoulder.
"I'm glad."

Chapter Eight

A week later, John pulled a blazing marshmallow from the fireplace. Blowing it out, he laid it on a graham cracker held by Christine and loaded with chocolate. She grinned, first at him and then at Tyler. "This will have to be your last," she said to her son before handing him the squishy treat.

The boy's face was liberally dotted with sticky mess. "But, Mom!"

"She's right, you know," John said, backing up Christine. "We wouldn't want you getting a bellyache. Not so soon before Christmas."

Tyler eagerly dug into his s'more while Mason ate his—complete with paper plate, but minus the chocolate—in the corner. John took in the cheery scene, acknowledging he hadn't had this much fun in months. Heck, maybe even in years. The afternoon spent outdoors with Christine and Tyler had been filled with happy hill rides and gleeful shouts. On the way back to the truck they'd had an impromptu snowball fight, and John had been mightily impressed by Christine's strong throwing arm. She'd invited him over for lunch the next day to compensate for whipping his tail in the competition. The next few days were lost in a blur of chats over coffee and prolonged Lego games with Tyler.

Now, here they were, all huddled up indoors beside a roaring fire and after a dinner of homemade stew. *It's like stepping into a greeting card,* John thought, his eyes lingering on Christine. She was beautiful in the firelight and the more he was around her, the more he wanted to be with her. She was captivating and sincere, and she had a sense of humor he appreciated. They could talk about everything in the world or nothing at all, just sitting in companionable silence. She was just as much fun as Carlos to be around, though John was betting she was a better kisser. Not that he'd be comparing the two, it was just odd for John to consider that a person could appeal to him in a womanly way and also act like a best friend. John was longing to get more than friendly with Christine. During their few moments alone, he'd actually considered making a move, but he'd stopped himself, weighing the impact on Tyler.

If things deepened between him and Christine, what would that mean? He clearly couldn't lead her on by engaging in some casual fling, when the outcome might be devastating for them all. Christine was loving yet firm with Tyler, and naturally a very protective mom. She wouldn't want to expose the boy to any fallout from a short-term affair any more than John would.

"When does Santa come again?" Tyler asked, still munching.

"Not until you're fast asleep," Christine answered.

"Did you ask for something special?" John asked the boy.

"Mommy says it's best to let life surprise you."

"Does she now?"

Christine blushed mightily under John's appreciative perusal. She really was lovely that way. It seemed to embarrass her that any man might cast an admiring eye her way. John wasn't sure how any guy in his right mind could stop himself.

Christine stood, collecting cooking supplies. "Ty, you'd best head upstairs and wash up. It's getting late and tomorrow is a big day." She turned to John. "Will you excuse me a minute while I tuck him in?"

"Maybe I should get going," John said, standing as well.

"No, don't." Her expression softened. "What I mean is, please stay. I won't be but a minute."

"Well, all right. Just for a bit."

Tyler twisted his lips and surveyed them both.

"Is John sleeping over?" he asked his mom.

John felt heat scorch the back of his neck as Christine flushed red.

"Oh no, honey," she sputtered quickly. "That's not what I meant."

Tyler stuck out his bottom lip. "Why can't he sleep over? He can stay in my room."

John smiled kindly at the child. "Maybe some other time, little buddy. Okay?"

"Promise?" Tyler asked, his face lighting up.

"We'll talk about it later," Christine said firmly, herding him toward the stairs. "Now come on, up to bed with you!"

Tyler turned with disappointment and slowly climbed each step.

Mason slunk out of the corner and stealthily followed after him.

"Mason, get back down here," John ordered.

The dog turned his head with a petitioning look.

"Please?" Tyler pleaded. "Just for a little while?"

When Christine came back downstairs she found the great room spotless. She entered the kitchen to find John drying the last of the dinner dishes.

"How nice," she exclaimed with surprise. "You really didn't have to."

"I have a skill set," he said. "Just because I'm a male that doesn't mean I don't know my way around the kitchen."

John didn't have to remind Christine what sex he was. Every time he centered his blue gaze on hers, she remembered through and through. He was so capable at so many things it sent her heart awhirl. She just bet the women were after him in this tiny town, probably in all of greater Burlington too. Not just the coeds, either. Adult women, single ones, widows, and divorcees. John was intelligent, handsome, and kind. Just the sort of man it was easy to envision spending more time with.

This past week had been like a dream. Christine hated the thought that her vacation would soon be over and that this wonderful existence would end. But that's what getaways were for, stepping back from your normal routine. She couldn't hope to have anyone as wonderful as John in her life for the long term. She'd found her Prince Charming once and real life didn't grant a lot of second chances. So she'd determined to enjoy this moment while she could. Being around John felt good, so relaxed and natural. Who knew? Maybe they could keep up after this trip, sort of like long-distance friends? Christine frowned at the thought of leaving John behind for another woman to snap up as a boyfriend, but she had no doubt that it would happen over time.

"My cooking's not that bad," John said with a laugh.

She met his eyes, realizing he'd been expounding on his culinary talents, and she'd missed every word. "I'm sure it's delicious, every bite."

"Really?" he said with a grin. "I never figured you for Cajun food. I'll have to make something for you sometime."

The way he said it was almost like he was in denial that she was leaving too. Would they just go on like this, then? Carrying on like congenial neighbors until it was time for her and Ty to board their plane? What else could Christine expect? Getting involved with John romantically would prove a mess. It would be bad for Tyler to become attached if things were not to work out. Christine felt a twisting in her gut, worrying that she'd already done the wrong thing in having them spend so much time with John. But, as long as Tyler understood the truth, that they were merely friends, would that ultimately matter? It was good to have friends in the world. Isn't that what she always told Ty? The more the merrier?

"Would you like me to open some wine?" John asked, looking and sounding a little puzzled.

Christine shook off her reverie, embarrassed at having been so consumed by her own thoughts. "That would be terrific," she said, feeling as if having a drink was a fine idea. She was getting overwrought, making too much out of nothing. Perhaps a glass of wine might calm her nerves enough to help her enjoy the rest of the pleasant evening with a terrific guy. "I'll grab a bottle from the bar in the great room," she said. "Would you like red or white?"

"What are you in the mood for?"

Christine knew he didn't mean it as a double entendre, but she felt herself blushing just the same. If circumstances were different and she and John starting an actual courtship, she could envision herself being in the mood for all sorts of things, not the least of which might involve John bringing his mouth to hers. She envisioned running her hands across his broad, muscular chest and slowly unbuttoning his shirt, hearing him moan. Christine gulped. "I'm partial to reds," she said with a squeak. She walked over to the built-in wine rack and rummaged clumsily through the bottles, reading labels and finding two varieties. "What sounds best? A cabernet sauvignon or merlot?"

"Let's have the merlot," he said, approaching from the kitchen.

"Do you think you can grab a corkscrew from the drawer by the sink?" she asked, needing an extra moment to collect herself. Christine smoothed out her hair and adjusted her sweater, hoping the five pounds she'd gained these past two years wouldn't put him off. Not that she was interested in turning him on. God, she was a mess.

He returned seconds later as Christine made for the kitchen, wine bottle in hand. They surprised each other on the threshold, nearly colliding.

"Whoops!" Christine exclaimed, almost dropping the bottle.

John steadied her shoulders in his strong hands. "Are you okay?"

Christine stared into brilliant blue eyes, then looked heavenward toward the mistletoe dangling above them. She met his gaze again, her cheeks, neck, and chest on fire. If she hadn't just been thinking about it, perhaps she wouldn't feel so much like a kid caught with her hand in the cookie jar. The only cookie here was about six feet tall and stood right in front of her. She found herself longing to take a bite.

"Christine?" he questioned uncertainly. Slowly, his eyes traveled north. He released her, stepping back.

"It's just a silly old tradition," she said, affecting a laugh.

John tilted his chin. "Not so silly, really."

"No," Christine said, swallowing hard. What had she been about to do? Tackle him to the floor? Maybe that wouldn't have been necessary. She could have stripped his jeans off right here, and…

"Shall I pour?" he asked, his complexion crimson from the neck up.

"Please." she said, catching her breath on the word. She had to get a grip. She would absolutely die if John had a clue about what she'd been thinking. He obviously wasn't interested in becoming physical. This week had provided ample opportunity for John to make a move after Ty had been tucked in bed, yet he hadn't acted on it. And it was a good thing, too. *Keeping things at arm's length is precisely what I want,* she thought, forcing a smile.

John poured them each a glass of wine and set the bottle on the dining room table. "Say," he said, noting her sketches, "are these yours?"

Christine had been so intent on serving their big bowls of stew by the fire, she'd completely forgotten she'd left these out from earlier in the afternoon. "They're just a couple of rough drafts. Something I'm working on."

"Well, I think they're fantastic" he said admiringly. "Really, Christine. When you said you wanted to start your own line, I had no idea. You've got serious talent."

"Thanks. I'd like to think so. At least enough to get something of my own going someday."

"I don't doubt it for a moment." He raised his wineglass to hers. "I have faith in you. Faith that you can pretty much accomplish anything you want to."

She clinked his glass, her heart light. John was so kind and accepting. His encouraging words meant the world to her. She was finally starting to recover from her earlier urge to ravage him. She must have been tipsy, thinking unclearly. When it was clear he meant to be only on platonic terms.

He lifted one of her drawings and studied it closely. "You know what you need?" he asked, looking up. "A business plan."

"A what?"

"A business plan," he said firmly. "A way to plot how to get from point A to point Z."

Christine hesitated. Of course she wanted to do it… eventually. Ever since John had first suggested starting her own company, she'd been considering her options. But it was a far-off dream, some nebulous fantasy. Nothing she could work on concretely at the moment. Starting her own line as a writer was ambitious enough. "I don't know," she began, "that involves a lot of time and effort. And right now, things are complicated. There's my present job… There's Ty…"

He eyed her astutely. "Hmm, yes. I see."

"What do you see?"

"Just that you're not ready, but that's okay. When you're ready, you'll know it."

Everyone needed long-term goals and this one was fun to think about. It didn't have to be this year, or even next... *Christine White Originals,* yes, that had a ring to it. Christine met John's gaze. "The future is long."

"It is indeed," he said with a grin.

Chapter Nine

As they sat by the fire enjoying their wine, John noted a CD on an end table. He picked it up with pleased surprise. "*A James Taylor Christmas*. Hey, is this yours?"

"In my mind I'm going to Carolina," she said with a smile that made him want to drop everything and go there with her. John liked James Taylor, but probably hadn't listened to his music in years.

"Mind if I put it on?" he asked.

"Sure. The stereo's right over there," she said, pointing to a cabinet near the bar.

"What's Christmas Eve without music?"

"You're right," she agreed. "We should have thought of it sooner."

John inserted the CD and a sappy yet sexy rendition of *Baby It's Cold Outside* began to play. "An oldie but goodie," he said.

"With a new twist."

Rich dark waves spilled to her shoulders as her cheeks took on a gentle glow. She was gorgeous in that pretty white sweater and jeans, her deep brown eyes sparkling in the soft light. Outside the windows, snow fell lightly, gently streaking the darkness. It was John's best Christmas Eve in recent memory. Maybe ever.

"You look really nice tonight," he said, his voice growing raspy. "Beautiful."

"Thanks," she said, her eyes locked on his. "I was just thinking that you look great too."

John sensed inside that he shouldn't do it, but an even louder inner voice said he'd be a fool to stop himself. Here he was, alone with a gorgeous woman on Christmas Eve, and John could think of only one thing he wanted—to close the distance between them. He'd been longing to hold her all week, and now he had the perfect excuse. He approached her and set down his wine. "Care to dance?"

John held out his hand and she took it, letting him guide her off the sofa and into his arms. She was so warm and feminine against him, the light scent of her wildflower perfume in the air. Firelight cast shadows on the wall as they gently swayed to the music. John pulled her close and she sighed softly, while his heart beat like big kettledrum. He had the feeling he was falling, sinking into depths he'd never known. As long as she went there with him, he didn't care if they ever came back.

At last, the CD ended and she looked up. There was a longing in her eyes, deeply beautiful. John led her to the threshold separating the great room from the kitchen. His voice was husky with desire as he spoke below the mistletoe.

"It's not such a silly tradition."

"No…" she said, tilting up her chin.

John brought his mouth to hers and kissed her sweetly at first, and then with the all-consuming passion he'd restrained these past several days. He wrapped her in his embrace and she moaned, molding into him. That was all the encouragement he needed to cradle her head in his hands and deepen his kisses, his hands eager to explore her body. She was all woman, and she was all his. He ached to carry her to the sofa and drive home that point, making her cry out with pleasure and delight.

"Mommy!" a small voice called.

Tyler bounded down the steps, Mason barking loudly and following after him.

John and Christine broke their embrace as John hitched his belt and Christine quickly straightened her sweater. Tyler sensed their interaction and halted his descent. "Oh," he said, absorbing the scene.

"Ty!" Christine said, flushed. "What are you doing up?"

"I heard something outside."

"It was probably just the wind," Christine told him.

"No," Ty protested. "I think it was Santa and his reindeer!"

John and Christine exchanged glances.

"We'd better go and check," he said.

Christine and John leaned out the bedroom window, spying nothing but a craggy old tree scraping the shutter.

"It was just an old oak, little fellow," John said reassuring Tyler. "I'm sure he didn't mean any harm." Christine's heart warmed at how natural it seemed for John to interact with her boy. He really was very good with children, with Ty in particular.

Tyler's face fell with disappointment. "Are you sure it wasn't Santa?"

"Santa hasn't gotten here yet," Christine said.

"And he might not come," John said, forcing a stern look, "if you don't go back to sleep."

Tyler snuggled down under the covers, pulling them up to his chin.

"I'd probably better hit the road," John told Christine.

"Are you sure?" She desperately didn't want him to go, but knew deep inside that he should. She couldn't exactly ask him to stay the night, not with Ty in the house. It wouldn't be right. Maybe it wouldn't even be right for her. They were leaving in less than a week. As wonderful as John's kisses were—and they'd been knee-melting terrific—it was likely better for Christine to not get in any deeper. If he kissed her again the way he'd done under the mistletoe, they might not be able to stop things there.

Blue eyes sparkled with understanding. "I think my leaving's for the best, don't you?"

She knew he was right, so she didn't argue. John mussed Tyler's hair and told him good night before heading for the door.

"We still on for tomorrow at five?" he asked Christine. "Christmas dinner at my place?"

"We wouldn't miss it for the world," she said with a happy smile.

Chapter Ten

The bright sun beat a path through the windows as wrapping paper littered the floor. Christine sat on the colorful hooked rug by the fire, helping Ty construct his Lincoln Log tower. He'd been as happy as a clam to learn Santa had brought him his own set, one he could take back to Chicago. He'd gotten a huge assortment of Legos too. That Santa really knew his stuff. Christine's cell rang and she nabbed it off the coffee table.

"Still snowing up there?" It was Ellen's voice on the other end of the line.

"Not at the moment," Christine answered cheerily. She was having the best New England Christmas. "But it never stops for long."

"That's good," Ellen said, "because I need somewhere to cool off."

"What?"

"A truly wicked sunburn," she continued in a pitiful tone.

"Oh my gosh! How did that happen?"

"Let's just say Emilio and I spent some time at the beach." She lowered her voice and spoke with a mysterious edge. "A… very… private… beach."

"Didn't you use protection?" Christine asked in shock.

"Of course we did! But not sunscreen."

Christine blinked at Tyler, opting to take her conversation to a more confidential locale. She stood, walking out of his earshot, then whispered into the phone. "Ellen, oh my God. You're burnt *everywhere*?"

"Some parts more than others," she quipped. "But that's neither here nor there. I'm calling to tell you my time in the sun is done."

"What do you mean?"

"Emilio and I weren't as compatible as I thought. He had a much harder time taking a tanning. And that says a lot, considering I didn't do so well... In any case, I'm calling to tell you the happy news! I'm coming up to relieve you in Vermont!"

Christine swallowed hard, staring at Tyler. They were finally settling in. Now clearly wasn't the time to walk away. They had three more days on their agenda. Besides, they had Christmas dinner plans. "Ellen, I really don't think that's necessary. Ty and I are doing just great holding down the fort."

"Of course, I don't mean to push you out completely. You can go home any time you want. Just make room for one more!"

Christine sighed and ran her fingers through her hair. "When were you thinking of arriving?" she asked weakly.

"At four. I'm calling from the airport, as a matter of fact."

"Four *today*?" Christine spouted in a panic. She'd been looking forward to an intimate evening at John's place. She hadn't planned on bringing along her brash best friend.

"I don't eat that much," Ellen said, affronted. "Frankly, Christine, I'm surprised at you. I didn't think you and Ty would... Wait a minute! Hold the phone!" she cried, her tone brightening. "Is this about the sexy professor?"

"Ellen!"

"I knew it! You finally went out, didn't you?"

"Actually, we stayed in."

"That sounds even better! So… out with it! Is he some kind of dynamite kisser?"

"Ellen!"

"Hmm, I see. No time for that yet. Well, no matter, sweetheart. Goodness knows I want you to have a love life way more than the next gal. I won't get in your way."

John laid three elegant place settings on the sturdy handmade table while Carlos heckled him from nearby. "I can't believe you'd disinvite your best friend on earth from his favorite holiday meal."

John wryly twisted his lips. "But you've always criticized my Indian pudding."

"That's because it's a little lumpy."

"Is not!"

"Is too. Although the Cornish hens always come out well," Carlos added thoughtfully.

"Thanks, Carlos. You're a pal." Mason followed him excitedly, repeatedly knocking his legs with a huge rawhide bone that sported a large red ribbon on at one end. "Mason, please. Will you just *sit*?" The dog sat immediately and John nearly tumbled over him.

Carlos smirked and got back to business. "So? Does she have any friends?"

"You mean, mature female friends?"

"No, I mean ones her age."

"Keep dreaming."

"What? Women find me attractive."

"That, my friend, is one of life's great mysteries."

"You're just jealous because you can't grow one of these," Carlos said stroking his beard.

"Could too. If I wanted to look like an old billy goat."

"Hey!"

John's cell rang and he held up a hand.

"Christine," he said cheerfully. "Well, hello. Uh huh… Uh huh… I see."

He stared at Carlos, who eyed him suspiciously.

"No, I don't think that would be a problem," John continued into the receiver. "In fact, it will work out fine!"

He pressed End Call and Carlos implored, palms up, "What gives?"

John shot him an enigmatic grin. "Let's just say it's your lucky day."

Chapter Eleven

A few hours later, John opened his front door to greet the trio, with Carlos and Mason at his side. Dusk had settled outdoors and it was snowing once more. Christine entered first, radiantly beautiful in a red Christmas scarf. "Welcome! Welcome to all of you," John said, greeting Christine with a hug. He patted Tyler on the shoulder and turned toward Christine's slightly senior friend. The attractive redhead was slender and fit, with a russet glow about her. "You must be Ellen," John said, extending his hand.

"Professor John Steadman!" she exclaimed, pulling him into a bear hug. She winced, the moment they made contact, her skin seemingly bruising in the embrace. "I feel like we're old friends." John raised his brow at Carlos, who repressed a grin. "Let me introduce you to Carlos Dominguez," he said, pulling back.

Carlos took her hand, turning on his Old World charm. *"Encantado,"* he said, laying his accent on thick.

Ellen preened like a peacock. *"Igualmente,"* she returned in nearly flawless Spanish.

Carlos addressed Christine next. "Great to see you again. You're looking well."

"Thanks, Carlos. You too. Merry Christmas," she said with a smile.

"Well, come on in! Come on in, everybody. In— and out of the cold."

The happy group strode toward the living room, Tyler with a bundle of packages in hand. "Can I put these under the tree?" he asked, Mason tagging along beside him.

"Under the tree's just fine," John said.

Before long, they were enjoying a scrumptious dinner John had cooked completely from scratch. *Is there no end to his talents?* Christine wondered. The ranch-style house was tastefully decorated for a bachelor pad, with upscale artwork hung on the walls. It was nicely done up for the holidays. A tall balsam fir nestled by the bay window, adorned with twinkling lights and a smattering of simple, yet elegant, ornaments. Carlos was in the midst of regaling them with business school stories.

"And that's when I said to Santa, 'That wasn't a signature line, it was an escape clause!'"

Ellen giggled with delight. Christine swore the evening had taken a decade off of her already youthful complexion, or perhaps it was the bright red hue on her cheeks inspired by an overexposure to the sun. "Carlos, what a great story. Have you ever thought of becoming a writer?"

"Oh, I'd say the folks at the business school find me verbose enough."

"It's true," John deadpanned. "We don't want to encourage him."

John stood to clear the dishes and Christine got to her feet as well.

"Let me help," she said with a soft smile.

Ellen and Carlos exchanged glances. "We'll come too," Ellen said, as they both made an effort to stand.

"No, please," John replied. "You two stay here and keep Tyler company. You all done with your food?" he asked the boy.

"Yeah, thanks! I've never eaten a whole chicken before."

Adults chuckled all around as John and Christine slipped into the kitchen.

Christine deposited dishes in the sink, thinking how much fun she was having. John wasn't only good in the kitchen, he was a great host too. "It was a wonderful dinner. You're some kind of cook."

"I've a few years to practice," he said, carrying a platter over.

Suddenly, they were face-to-face in the small space.

Christine froze, trapped in his gaze. He was a marvelous man. Gracious too. "It was really nice of you to include Ellen so last-minute."

"She and Carlos seem to be hitting it off."

"Boy, do they ever."

"I think it's cute."

"And so unexpected."

"You certainly weren't expecting Ellen to show up."

"No."

Christine searched his eyes. "Sometimes life delivers things we don't plan."

"I like to think of them as pleasant surprises." John stepped closer, taking her in his arms just as Carlos and Ellen entered the kitchen.

"Oops!" Ellen said.

"We were just hoping to help serve dessert," explained Carlos. He massaged his beard as Tyler and Mason also entered the kitchen.

"What's going on?" Tyler asked, contorting his lips. "More *kissing*?"

Ellen and Carlos stared at each other while Christine and John flushed.

"Actually, Tyler," Carlos said to the child. "We were all just thinking it'd be a good idea for some of us to go and look at that Christmas tree."

"Yeah, right," Ellen piped in. "I believe there's a package or two with your name on it."

Tyler's face lit up. "Really? Whoohoo!"

As they departed, Christine heaved a sigh. "Great friends."

"World's best."

"What were we saying?"

"I don't know," he said, drawing closer. "Something about life's surprises?"

And boy, hadn't life surprised her with John. She hadn't realized until last night how much she cared about him. Judging by the way he'd kissed her under the mistletoe, he had feelings for her too.

"Sometimes what we least expect is the best, don't you think?" she said, looking up at him. "What I mean to say is…" Christine stood a bit straighter, gathering her courage. "John, this holiday has been great, the best ever. I could never have imagined it happening to me, but it has."

"What has?"

Heat swept from her temples to her toes as she locked on his gaze. "This… us, being here with you. Having you fit in so well with me and Tyler. And, you know what? I'm happy, really happy, for the first time since I don't know when."

John swallowed hard and stared at her blankly. This was just what he had worried might happen. She was growing attached, more attached than he was ready for. John had seen the signs before and they'd always sent him running for the hills. He liked Christine, cared about her of course, but this was sounding really heavy. He'd made a hell of a mistake with that kiss when he would have done better to control himself. Now, she thought... Hell, he didn't even know what she thought. He only knew he didn't want to think about it. "Yes, well," he said after a pause. "It's been pretty terrific getting to know you all too."

There was an awkward silence during which they heard Ellen's melodious laughter from the next room. John lifted a bottle of wine from the counter. "I'm going to see if anyone needs a refill," he said, sounding like he might need one himself.

Christine quickly followed after him, thinking she could use a drink, too.

While the rest of the group seemed oblivious, Christine felt unsettled. She'd practically spilled her guts to John, and he'd basically said—nothing. Even now, he sat apart from her as if something were amiss. Maybe she was letting her insecurities get the best of her. She hadn't felt close to a man in forever, and hadn't even kissed anyone since Dan. And now, here she'd gone acting like some giddy teenager engaged in her first crush. She'd probably frightened John a little with her admission, but why wouldn't he feel good that he'd helped make her happy? She studied him, hands clasped at his knees as he leaned forward with a congenial smile, watching Tyler opening his gifts. Was he avoiding meeting her eyes, or was she imagining it?

Tyler dug into another package, Mason snoozing contentedly at his side. "Nintendo! Oh boy! Thanks, Auntie Ellen. Mommy said I couldn't have one."

Ellen shot Christine a look. "Sorry."

"It's fine," Christine said, wishing everything really was okay.

Carlos wrapped his arm around Ellen's shoulder. "That's what Aunties are for," he whispered gruffly, but not quietly enough so the others didn't hear him.

Ellen grimaced at Christine, but Christine couldn't tell if it was in apology or because Carlos's embrace hurt her.

Carlos studied Ellen with concern. "Are you all right?" he asked, lifting his arm. "Is this bothering—?"

"Not much," she said, snuggling against him in encouragement. "Just a touch of sunburn."

"Maybe I can help with some cold cream later?" he said softly in her ear.

"Oh!" Ellen responded with delighted surprise. She locked on Carlos's gaze and blinked. "That would be nice, very nice indeed."

John leaned forward, lifting a small box from an end table. "Wait," he told Tyler, who was organizing his gifts. "There's one more." He glanced at Christine, his complexion ruddy. "This one's for the two of you."

"Thanks," she said, accepting the package. She felt bad that she hadn't brought anything for him other than a bottle of wine. But, in light of how skittish he was acting, maybe her omission was for the best. "Ty? You want to do the honors?"

The child grinned and slid the silky ribbon from the gift, peeling back the wrapping. He dug in the box and extracted a tiny toboggan tree ornament. "Look Mommy," Tyler proclaimed. "It's a sled! Just like we went on!"

"Just a little something for you to remember Vermont by."

"Oh how cute," Ellen chimed in.

Emotion welled in Christine's throat. Of all the moments they'd shared with John, that was one she'd never forget. "It's wonderful," she said softly. "Thank you."

"John took me and Mommy sledding!" Tyler informed the others.

"So I *heard*," Ellen said with a knowing look.

"Does this mean we'll get a real Christmas tree next year?" Tyler asked.

"Christine doesn't believe in Christmas trees," Ellen told Carlos.

"Really?" Carlos asked with surprise.

"That's not true," Christine protested. "I just haven't gone to the trouble these past…" Now, it was her turn to avoid John's gaze. "… few years."

"Well…" John clapped his hands together and glanced around. "Maybe next year things will be different."

The room was silent as all eyes fell on him. John stared first at Carlos and Ellen, then at Tyler and Mason by the tree. Finally, he looked at Christine. "For you, Christine. I meant, for you," he said, his voice cracking. He stood suddenly, sweat beads dotting his brow. "I'm going to grab some water. Anybody else want a glass?"

"I'll come help," Carlos said, getting to his feet.

John leaned into the counter and took a long drink.

"What is it, amigo," Carlos asked. "What's wrong?"

"Suddenly, I don't feel so hot."

"No joke. You look like you've seen a ghost."

John gradually met his gaze. "I have, Carlos. The Ghost of Christmas Future, and it's too much. It's all too much."

"What's too much?"

"*This.* Old home week. Christine… Tyler… I just can't do it."

"Nobody's asked you to do anything, other than have them to dinner. As I recall, it was your invitation."

"Her best friend's here. You know they've been talking about me."

"That's what best girlfriends do!" Carlos reassured him. "They even weigh the merits of the UPS man, from what I hear."

John looked Carlos in the eye. "I heard from Mary Stewart."

"On the personnel committee?"

John nodded. "If I want it, the position's mine."

"That's awesome news. Congratulations."

"You know what this means. Long hours… extra meetings… Honestly, it's a good thing Christine and Tyler are going home."

Carlos cocked his chin. "Sometimes distance doesn't matter."

"And sometimes it's an excellent deterrent," John said firmly. "Just the right thing, at just the right time, before anyone's in too deep."

Carlos shook his head with a disapproving look. "And I thought the only chickens in this house were the ones you served for dinner."

Chapter Twelve

Christine and Ellen rode in the front of the SUV while Tyler slept soundly in his car seat in back. It had been a full and joyful day for her little boy; Christine was grateful for that at least. She kept her eyes on the road, trying not to think too hard about John's parting statement. Could she really have made such colossal mistakes that he didn't ever want to see her or Tyler again?

Ellen checked her lipstick in the driver's side mirror and fluffed her hair, lost in her own world. "I think the sexy professor's sweet on you," she said settling back in her seat. "*Maybe next year things will be different...?* That sounded promising!"

"You totally misread that, Ellen. I doubt that's what John meant at all."

"He's got the love bug for you, sister," Ellen stated authoritatively. "The love bug and it shows. That man wants you in his future."

"That man, as you call him, was only making conversation. Think about it Ellen. I'm in Chicago, he's in Vermont... Just how is that supposed to work?"

"I used to date a guy in New York."

"*Used to* being the operative phrase."

Ellen folded her arms across her chest. "As a girl who's got a date tomorrow, I don't appreciate your pessimism."

Christine turned toward her, pleased. "Carlos?"

"Isn't he gorgeous," Ellen asked with a sigh.

"I guess he's got a certain appeal," Christine said noncommittally. "So, where are you two going?"

"Snowmobiling!"

"Seriously?"

"What? It's not like bungee jumping. Though I'd be up for that too... What do you think? Too much to suggest for a second date?"

"How long are you planning on staying?"

"For the rest of the holiday, and you?"

"Our return flight's on the twenty-eighth. You know that, you arranged it."

"Oh right, right. Sorry. I forgot." Ellen fiddled with her purse, sneaking out her cell to check for messages. "Do you think Carlos has been married before?"

"From what I hear, twice."

"Third time's the charm," Ellen quipped merrily.

"You two just met!"

"I know, I know... Don't take me so seriously. Heavens!" She frowned, tucking away her cell. "So... When are you seeing John again?"

Christine's lips took a downward turn as she fought the burn in her heart. "I'm not."

Ellen reached out and touched her arm. "What happened?"

Christine felt a tear escape her and she stealthily stroked it back, hoping Ellen hadn't seen. "I should never have gotten involved. I knew from the beginning where things would end."

"Did John say something to you?" Ellen asked with concern. "When we were leaving, I mean?"

Christine pressed her lips together steeling her emotions.

"Have a nice flight," she said, battling the sting of her tears.

"Oh Christine, I'm so sorry. I had no idea, hon. Honestly, none. John seemed like such a nice guy. I was hopeful, really hopeful—for the first time in a long while—that you were finally getting your life back."

Christine collected herself, wiping her cheeks with her coat sleeve. "My life's in Chicago," she said with more resolve than she felt.

"I know, and mine is too." Ellen set her jaw, weighing her own insecurities. "I'm not fooling myself with Carlos. The two of us are old enough to know what the score is. That doesn't mean we can't enjoy a little fun while we've both got some life left."

Christine forced a smile. "Oh Ellen, I'd say you've got plenty of life left. Maybe even more than Carlos can handle."

Ellen laughed, the tension in the air lightening. "Thanks," she said. "I try."

Later that night, Christine locked herself away in her room, her heart breaking. All night long she'd held it in. Fear started as a gentle roll, cresting the wave of her emotions, the moment John gave her that deer-in-the-headlights look in the kitchen. By the time they were saying good-bye, hope had sunk in the well of silence between them. It wasn't that they didn't talk. Discomfort sprung instead from all that went unsaid. There was no discourse on keeping in touch, or John seeing them off to the airport. The holiday had come, then—boom—it was done, just as suddenly as fireworks exploding on the Fourth of July. But here it was Christmas… *Christmas*… and all its twinkling lights had faded for her, it seemed.

There'd been a time when the whole world had looked promising. She'd had a handsome young officer on her arm and they'd been expecting their first child. Dan had sworn he'd never leave her, but, due to the cruelty of fate, he had. She'd never believed she'd love again, or even meet another guy who'd catch her eye. Now here she was more painfully aware of being alone than she'd ever been.

Christine sank to the carpet, her back to the door, arms folded around her knees. "Oh Dan," she said, doubling forward with her sobs. "I miss you so much."

A light rapping came at the door. "Everything okay in there?" It was Ellen from the other side, her voice tinged with worry.

Christine sucked in a breath, her throat raw. "Yes, Ellen!" she called back. "Just fine. Merry Christmas."

Ellen hesitated before replying, concern clear in her voice. "Merry Christmas. Sleep tight."

Christine listened to her footsteps fade away, then folded her face in her hands. She'd been acting like a fool. Crushing on a man who lived hundreds of miles away and clearly had no interest in falling in love, much less having a family. She'd been crazy to believe there could be more to her relationship with John than just a simple two-week affair. Maybe it was good that she was heading back to Chicago, where she could put her real world in order and ensure it all made sense. In the meantime, she'd need to put on a brave face for these last few days and make the most of this vacation for little Ty. He was the main reason she came here after all, not to create delusional fantasies about her achieving a *happily ever after*.

Christine dropped her forehead to her knees and let the tears come quietly, as winds beat against the storm shutters. It was snowing harder now, almost as fiercely as it had on the day they arrived. But nothing could match the chill that settled deep in her soul to ravage her aching heart.

Chapter Thirteen

John fixed his brow in concentration, spreadsheets strewn across the tabletop around him. His printer spewed out more papers as he typed busily at his laptop, ignoring the doorbell the first time it chimed. It rang again and Mason barked. John looked up with a start to find sun streaming in through the windows. He stood wearily and walked to the door. Pulling it open he spied Carlos dressed for the cold. Beyond him, Ellen smiled and waved from a truck loaded with winter fishing gear.

"Carlos!" John said with surprise. "I thought you had a date."

"I do." Carlos grinned broadly. "We're just stopping by to be sure that you won't join us."

Mason tried to spring out the door, but John stopped him. "Not today, buddy," he said to his dog.

"Come on now," Carlos prodded. "It will be fun."

John slowly shook his head. "Thanks, but I can think of lots of things I'd rather do than be the third wheel on a fishing expedition."

Carlos's jowls sagged with disappointment.

"Besides," John continued, backing into his house. "I've got work to do."

Carlos leaned forward and grabbed him by the shirtsleeve. "Amigo," he rasped under his breath. "You don't understand. I've never taken a city woman fishing!"

"Oh, no you don't…" John chuckled and started closing the door. "You got yourself into this; you get yourself out."

Carlos stared at him with pleading eyes. "I'll give you half my catch."

"Half of nothing is zero. We don't need our accountant friends to tell us that."

Carlos stuck his foot in the door before John could close it. "When have I ever not been there for you?"

"Lots!"

"Okay, maybe that's true. But here's the chance for you to be the bigger man."

"Good-bye Carlos," John said, kicking his foot out of the doorjamb.

John shook his head at Mason as they walked back to the table. "And people say *women* are complicated."

Back at Winterhaven, Christine carted the last of their suitcases downstairs.

"I can't believe we're really leaving," she said, glancing around the comfortable space that, in such a little while, already felt like home.

"We'll miss it here," Tyler said, holding Jasper close.

Christine smiled tenderly at her son. "At least Santa brought you some Lincoln Logs to take home."

"Yeah. That's cool," he said his face brightening.

Christine gave the house one last perusal. Everything was pretty much in order, other than a few odds and ends. She didn't really want to put all the things away in the event Ellen might need them. She'd even bought some extra wine when she'd purchased her replacements, thinking Ellen and Carlos might open a few bottles later.

Ellen had called her cousin in London to gently break the news about her blooming affair with Carlos. To her happy surprise, her cousin, by now involved with a handsome Frenchman, was delighted. Carlos was nice enough, she'd stated, just a little too used to *taking a walk on the wild side* for her taste. Christine sighed, glad that life had a way of working out much of the time.

"I guess we'll let Auntie Ellen do the rest of the picking up."

"Why isn't she flying back with us?" Tyler wanted to know.

"Your Auntie Ellen had a few things to take care of," she said, thinking of Carlos.

About ten miles away, Ellen stood in designer boots perched over a fishing hole cut in the ice. She couldn't believe she was doing this! Fishing in the wilds of Vermont! It was positively to-die-for adventuresome, particularly with one hot Latino along. His tender ministrations to her scorched skin had worked wonders. While she wasn't exactly as good as new, she had improved enough to enjoy his attentions—and layer into this bulky coat.

She felt a tug on her line and squealed with delight. "I've got one! Carlos, I think I've got one!"

"Looks like a big one, too," he said, stepping up behind her.

The beast tugged harder, threatening to pull her in. "Whoa… oh! Carlos!" she yelped, starting to freak just a little. Maybe it was enormous and had teeth! Ellen wasn't sure whether they had piranhas up here, but decided now was not the time to find out.

"Hold it steady," Carlos offered. "Let me help you."

He sidled up behind her, positioning his legs on either side of hers and wrapping his firm grip around the pole before them. She almost swore she felt his pole pressing up against her backside. She squirmed with excitement, suddenly too hot in her heavy clothing.

"This isn't working out so badly," he said in a sexy whisper that nearly melted the ice beneath them. If she weren't so dearly afraid for her life, she might have found herself turned on. For now, Ellen just hoped to live until lunchtime.

The line yanked forward as they wrestled with their footing. "Do they have sharks up here? Great whites?" Ellen asked. She dug her heels into the slick surface below her, thinking maybe practicality should have trumped fashion just this once.

Carlos settled her hips and bottom against him with one arm, to keep her from sliding, then said in a commanding voice, "We're going to take that sucker for what he's worth. You ready?"

As long as he was in charge and they weren't going under, Ellen was prepared to do anything Carlos said. She nodded, grimacing at the strain of holding the pole that arched over in their grip.

"When I say go…"

"What happens on *go*?" she asked, glancing quickly over her shoulder.

His eyes danced with mirth as he gave her a peck on the cheek. Her skin tingled at the brush of his beard and she saw a flash of bright light. Either she was dizzy from the contact or going snow-blind. "We pull that baby out of the water." He leaned back a bit and added with a chuckle. "Though something tells me it's an awfully big baby.

"Ready…" he started, strengthening his hold on both her and the pole. "Set…"

Ellen's heart thundered at the thought she was about to do it. Something so recklessly primitive as catching a fish!

"Go!" Carlos shouted, wrenching back with all his might. Ellen gave it everything she had, yanking hard. The monster strained against them. They pulled, it tugged… they pulled, it tugged. Then finally they pulled harder, and—*wham*! Ellen and Carlos fell back in a heap, with her landing squarely on top of him.

"Are you all right?" he asked, gripping her breasts through her coat as she stared up into a clear, blue sky.

"I think so," she said, spinning over on top of him. Six feet away, the most enormous fish she'd seen in her life flip-flopped on its side beyond their tackle box.

Ellen grinned. "We got him!" she shouted, happily pounding Carlo's chest with her gloves. "By God, we got him!"

Carlos laughed with delight and pulled her toward him for a kiss. "Damn good fishing for a city woman."

Christine and Tyler made their way through the busy crowd at the airport, dragging their rolling carry-on bags behind them. They were almost to security when Christine heard a distant cry. "Christine! Wait!"

Tyler turned first. "Mommy! Look!"

She spun on her heels to find John sprinting toward them in his Carolina sweatshirt, a large manila envelope in hand.

"Thank God I caught you." He leaned forward panting, hands resting on his thighs. "I thought I was too late."

Christine stared at him is disbelief. "What are you doing here?"

He huffed and puffed, still catching his breath. "I couldn't let you leave without this," he said, extending the manila envelop toward her.

"I'm not sure I understand. What is it?"

John caught his wind, straightening. "A business plan, Christine. This is it! A solution. A way to get from point A to point Z!"

She stared at him flatly unable to mask her disappointment. "Oh."

He appeared confused, thrown off guard. John ran his fingers through his short dark hair, settling his gaze on hers. "But this is what you've wanted. Your own line. Your own company, even. I…" He surveyed her once more, his cheeks sagging. "I thought that you'd be pleased."

"Pleased, John? When you didn't even bother to tell us good-bye? Just sort of dropped out of the picture? And now you suddenly appear with *this*." She eyed the envelope with disdain, causing him to flinch and step back.

He wrinkled his brow, pleading. "Won't you at least take a look? Glance over it on your flight?"

She'd spent these last three days trying to forget him. The last thing she needed to do was carry reminders home. "Thanks, but I've got to make plans for my life in Chicago."

"But this *is* for your life," he said, attempting once more to hand it over. "Christine, please…" He released the envelope, but she failed to grasp it, letting it fall to the floor. Tyler eyed them both uncertainly, then scooped it up.

Christine set her chin and willed it not to tremble. Here was this gorgeous man with whom she thought she'd made a personal connection, and all he cared about was cold, hard business. Perhaps he'd never felt anything for her at all, or for Tyler, either.

"Thanks for a swell New England vacation," she said, turning away and taking Tyler's hand. "It was nice knowing you." She walked her child toward security, the pain in her chest searing. After Christmas night, she didn't believe her heart could break again, but she'd been wrong.

Tyler looked sadly over his shoulder as they slipped away, milling in with the line passing through the security scanner. John couldn't stop the burn in his throat any more than he could the heat in his eyes. He'd thought she'd be happy to see him. Instead, she'd greeted him with chilling disdain. He'd spent untold hours on that plan, believing it was the best thing he could do for her. Wasn't helping her build the life she wanted the right thing? Her world was in Chicago; his life was here. There were no two ways about it.

John pursed his lips, recalling toboggan rides and warm nights by the fire… Little Tyler's *Whoohoo!* when he was thrilled about something. Then, there was the memory of Christine in his arms as they danced through the night, and his inward desire to never let her go. But the hard fact was that he couldn't hold on forever.

"You did *what*?" Carlos asked with disbelief when they met for coffee a few hours later. "Followed her all the way to the airport to deliver a *business plan*?"

"Come on, man," John said, feeling gloomy. "I thought that you, of all people, would understand what a gesture that was."

"No. What kind of gesture was it?"

"A very generous one! I put my heart and soul into that proposal!"

"Harrumph."

"What's that supposed to mean?"

"Let me guess. She wasn't exactly thrilled to see you."

"No, in fact she wasn't," John said, still reeling from the shock. "Frankly, she was pretty ticked off."

Carlos slowly shook his head then met John's eyes. "You know, for a very smart man, you can be a really big dummy sometimes."

"What are you driving at, Carlos. Just spill it."

"John, John… You meet this pretty single mom up here on vacation. You wine her and dine her and make her think something is possible…"

"Hang on just one second! She did every bit as much wining and dining as I did!"

"You're only proving my point."

"Which is?"

"You may not have wanted it to happen. By some Christmas miracle, maybe even the two of you didn't see it coming. But, one way or another, you and Christine were drawn to each other, found yourselves falling—"

"Precisely why I had to stop it!" John shot back. "Can't you see? That was the best thing—the right thing—for us both!"

Carlos slowly stroked his beard. "Was it?"

Mason, who'd been sitting at John's feet, shot him a dirty look.

"You," John admonished the dog, "stay out of it."

Chapter Fourteen

It was New Year's Eve in the elegant bistro. Carlos poured Ellen a glass of champagne as they sat at a romantic table for two.

"I'm having a hard time feeling festive with things ending so badly between John and Christine," she said.

Carlos took her hand. "I know, *querida*. But it's their business, and their problem to work out."

"What are the odds?"

"In love, everything's uncertain, yes?" He lifted her hand giving the back of it a kiss. "Sometimes you win, sometimes you lose. Then you head back to *go* and start all over again."

"That's just it," Ellen said with a worried frown. "I don't know if Christine will ever head back to *go* after this." She sipped from her champagne. "Where's John tonight?"

"Likely moping about his place with that old mutt of his," Carlos answered. "What do you think Christine's doing?"

Ellen sighed. "Probably sitting around in her apartment with Tyler, watching the ball drop on TV."

The two of them sat for a moment in silence.

"Do you think Christine will be okay?" Carlos asked with concern.

"Oh yeah, she'll bounce back. She's tough. I don't know about in the love department… but, otherwise, she'll get her life together. Christine always gets her life together. She's got to, right? She does it for Tyler." She pursed her lips and looked at him. "What about John?"

Carlos shrugged. "Tough as nails, too. He'll be fine."

But, by the way the two of them stared at each other, it was as if neither one believed it.

Carlos perused Ellen thoughtfully. "What time do you leave in the morning?"

"Ten o'clock."

"Then let's not let tonight go to waste," he said, clinking her glass.

Ellen smiled warmly, thinking what a rare and unexpected treat it was that the two of them had met. "To us," she said, toasting back.

"And to living in the moment, when the moment's right."

Tyler dozed in a large leather chair, a New Year's hat askew on his head, as Christine watch the ball drop in New York's Times Square on television. *Happy New Year, indeed.* She shared a silent toast with the air, then frowned. Everything felt wrong about how things had ended with John, but she hadn't really seen another way around it. What was she supposed to do? Fall at his feet with gratitude when he'd surprised her at the airport with that ridiculous plan?

She tapped her glass with her fingers, eying the manila envelop on the end table. What could be so hellfire important that he'd raced to catch them before they boarded their plane? *A way to get from point A to Z?* Well fine. John could keep his unsolicited advice, and Christine wished he had. Seeing him at the airport had just made things worse. She'd known he'd really hurt her, but hadn't understood how badly until he'd appeared at the last minute and caused her battered heart to hope. For an instant, she believed him to regret letting them go without so much as a word. But he'd shown no hint of remorse at all, only confusion in light of his damnable insistence that she read what he'd brought.

Christine drew a deep breath, steeling her emotions. She didn't need a sexy professor from New England anyway. She and Ty had done just fine before he'd come along, and would do great going forward without him. He could keep all that snow, and those tobogganing hills, the warm nights by the fire, and his dog. Christine sighed, recalling Tyler's joyful bonding with Mason. Maybe she'd have to get him a puppy. But not any time soon. There was enough going on in the balancing act between being a single mom and working.

She took another sip of champagne, weighing the demands of her job and all it entailed. The truth was that she'd been asking for more responsibility at work, but Ellen had been resistant. Perhaps it was true that Christine had seemed out of focus before, but the trip to Vermont had done her good. She sensed greater clarity now. While John had been wrong in many ways, most especially in the way he'd treated her, he actually was correct in assuming Christine wanted more for herself than what she currently had. She was capable of it too. She knew she could develop her own line, and had several ideas for interactive products with Internet potential as well. It would likely take time, but she was still relatively young, so time was on her side. John's prescient words came back to her like a haunting refrain. *The future is long…*

She set down her champagne and lifted the manila envelope, almost afraid of its contents. What if John's plan was more helpful than she'd imagined? She had enough of a level head to separate a business opportunity from a personal disappointment, didn't she? If she ultimately had a different path for herself in mind, wouldn't it make sense to think out the logical steps to achieving her goal now? She tentatively broke its seal, her heart pounding. It was just a stack of papers. So why did Christine have a premonition her whole life was about to change?

John flipped off the TV and set down the remote. On the coffee table before him, a bottle of champagne in bucket of ice sat untouched. He'd considered inviting one of his lady friends to join him for the evening, but somehow the thought of entertaining was distasteful. He didn't really want to have anyone else over when the only person he could think of was Christine. While it had never been a big deal before, being physical with a casual acquaintance suddenly didn't appeal to him. He'd only kissed Christine once, but their kissing session had felt as intimate as they come. She'd been so warm and willing in his arms, her flesh molding against his as their mouths melded. He'd never longed to make love to a woman more, slowly and tenderly, employing all of his manly talents. He knew he could treat her right, and would take every care to ensure her happiness in bed. Sadly, he hadn't done such a hot job of filling her with joy outside of it.

He glanced at Mason, still mad at him, on the other side of the room. The dog turned his back on John, sitting beside the Christmas tree.

"Come on, boy. You're not going to hold a grudge forever?"

Mason walked his paws forward, slinking into a lying position. After a few moments, John heard him gnawing and knew he'd locked onto his giant rawhide bone. John sagged forward, his elbows resting on his knees, head in hands. If he'd really done the right thing with Christine, then why was everybody here trying to make him feel like he'd done something terrible?

John thought back to Christine's admission in the kitchen. He *had* made her happy out of bed, but then he'd gone and blown it big-time. But she'd caught him so off guard, he hadn't known how to respond. What could he have said? That she made him happy too? John stared at the Christmas tree, mentally reliving every moment. Of course, she'd made him happy. She and Tyler both had, each in their own way. When he'd been with the two of them together, they'd been almost like a family. Although it had been pretend, he'd felt contented in that role. He'd just been so unfamiliar with the feeling, he hadn't known what it was.

John swallowed hard, thinking there'd been another emotion present, something deeply personal and just between him and Christine, but he'd been in denial of that as well. He had his hands full these days and building his career to consider besides. Despite the common myth of the easygoing life of the college professor, the hard truth was that competition in academia was exceedingly tough. You had to publish or perish, and keep forging ahead. John was an ambitious man who'd carved out a path for himself. His own dad had been an unsteady worker who was often unemployed and barely able to keep food on the table for John and his younger sister.

John had vowed at thirteen to work his way past that. And, from that first job tending the golf course at that upper-crust country club to his full graduate school scholarship, he had. Still, John believed he shouldn't become serious with any woman, or consider having a family, until he found himself in a financially stable position. He'd be damned if he was going to repeat the past, when he was capable of charting his own future. Of course, he was contemporary enough to understand his wife would have her own career, but that didn't negate the sense of responsibility that had been pounded into him each time he'd seen tears of desperation welling in his mother's eyes. Because his late dad had been unable to prepare for it, John was now making arrangements for his mom's welfare too. He also helped out his kid sister, as he was able. She was a single mom and putting herself through school besides. There was a lot on his plate, a hell of a lot more than Christine, or anyone else—including Carlos—knew.

John decided to open the champagne, thinking he might as well have a glass. There were so many emotions churning inside him, it was almost like he didn't know where to turn. *Man's best friend* had denied him, and it appeared his own heart had betrayed him too. He'd not even understood what he'd been feeling until now. And now, it was too late. The truth was that his promotion put him in a different place. Yes, he'd be working harder, but he'd also be making more money. *A lot more money,* he thought, popping the cork. It sprang forth in an arc as bubbles gurgled from the bottle. John picked up a cloth to wipe it, reaching forward for the cork on the floor. His fingers made contact with something else set back a little farther under the coffee table. What in Hades was that? John pinched the wooly fabric between his fingers, then slowly withdrew a bright red object from its stowaway perch.

Mason stood, turning toward him.

"Well, what do you know...?" John said aloud.

Ellen melted in Carlos's rapturous embrace at the airport. It was January first and her vacation had ended. "I'm not going to ask when I'm going to see you again," she said sadly.

Carlos pressed his forehead to hers. "Now you're hurting my feelings."

Ellen stared into warm brown eyes knowing she couldn't stand to say good-bye forever. "When's the last time you came to Chicago?"

"Nineteen seventy-nine."

"Then you're overdue!"

"I have a problem with that," Carlos said, pulling back.

"Oh?"

"My old college chum, the one I used to stay with..." he began seriously, "has moved away."

She knew what he was getting at, but couldn't resist teasing him. "I know some good hotels in the area."

Carlos feigned shock. "You wouldn't toss an old man out in the snow?"

Ellen kissed him soundly his bristly beard tickling.

"Call me," she said, breaking away.

Carlos beamed as she picked up her luggage and set it on the conveyor belt. He withdrew his cell from his pocket and waved it in her direction. "I've got your number!"

Chapter Fifteen

Christine sat at her drafting table intent on her sketch while classical music played in the background. All the Christmas decorations were tucked away, leaving her apartment with a neat array of modern furniture and clean open spaces. This drawing was whimsical and fun, with a family of snowmen tobogganing down a pine-studded hill. While there was computer software for graphic design, Christine preferred importing her hand-drawn illustrations into her layout program by using a scanner. This gave her the ability to create high-tech products with down-home appeal. It would take at least five years on her current income to save up enough to start her own company. In the meantime, she was determined to build a preliminary catalogue.

She took a sip of coffee as sunlight streamed through the windows. It was still windy outdoors, but the mid-January snow had abated despite the freezing temperatures. A vague sound buzzed upstairs and she heard something thumping down the steps. Christine looked up to see Tyler headed downstairs, his tiny cell in one hand, dog-eared Jasper in the other. "Good morning, Sunshine!" she called happily from her stool.

"Do I have school today?" he asked sleepily.

"Yes baby, you do. But first," she said, standing, "you're in for a treat."

"Huh?" he asked warily.

"I made homemade blueberry muffins."

He squinted his eyes. "You're cooking before dinner?"

Christine spurted a laugh and set a hand on her hip. "Your mom's a pretty capable woman."

He studied her for a prolonged beat. "I thought so, but wasn't sure."

He had such a way to fill her with confidence, Christine thought jovially. She was happy inside, happier than she'd been in a long time. Maybe she didn't need a college professor to make her feel it, but it likely had helped that he'd pointed the way. Until Christine went to Vermont, it was like a part of her lay dormant, just waiting to be reawakened. Though her initial parting from John had left a bitter taste in her mouth, Christine realized after a while that she was the type who used lemons to make lemonade. Perhaps knowing John had been bittersweet, but being with him while reconnecting with Tyler would pay dividends for months to come. She not only got along better with her son, she'd gained additional confidence in herself. Confidence that she could do anything she put her mind to, given enough time. *The future is long indeed,* she thought with a melancholy smile.

John waited in Ellen's office with Mason, hoping he wasn't being an egregious fool. But, the more he'd thought about it, the more right this step seemed. John wasn't a reckless man. He weighed everything carefully, considered all the angles. And every way he posed the question, the answer came up the same. His semester started on Tuesday and he'd put off coming here until the last minute, needing to ensure everything was in place.

John twisted Christine's red Christmas scarf in his hands, wishing with all his might that she'd be glad to see him. Both Ellen and Carlos had assured him she would. Then again, those two were turning out to be incurable romantics. He'd been pleasantly surprised by Carlos's sudden attachment to vivacious Ellen. He'd never seen the old boy fall quite so fast, or so hard. Of course, she seemed fairly well smitten with Carlos too. What serendipity that Ellen had joined Christine in Vermont at the last minute. Sometimes the fates really knew what they were doing.

John felt a rash of heat at his neck, realizing that this was the big time. He was more nervous now than when he'd defended his dissertation. He hoped he could turn that fear into a focused delivery. Yeah, he'd been a total jerk, and he knew it. He was fully prepared to apologize for it. Hell, even grovel. If that's what it took for Christine to give him half a chance.

Christine dropped Tyler at preschool and headed for the office. It was a little unusual for Ellen to call a personal meeting at nine o'clock. Generally her friend reserved individual conferences for after lunch. Mornings were good for settling in, answering phone calls and e-mails, and meeting with the general staff. Ellen also liked to give her people a few extra hours to polish any mock-ups they were working on before discussing them one-on-one. The funny thing was, as far as she knew, Christine didn't have anything specific to talk to Ellen about. Her projects were humming along fine and she'd kept her personal ambitions separate. Ellen didn't know she was planning to go out on her own, and keeping things to herself seemed the best policy right now. Given that Christine wouldn't be leaving the company tomorrow, there was no point in upsetting any applecarts with distant future plans.

Christine breezed into the lobby of her skyscraper building, her coat collar turned up against the cold. For the life of her, she wished she could recall where she'd left her favorite scarf, but she'd given up looking, thinking she must have forgotten it on the plane. She pressed the elevator button with a gloved hand, mentally going through a checklist of all she had to do today. The schedule was so tight, she wasn't sure she'd be able to make time for lunch. It was a good thing she and Tyler had shared a healthy breakfast. It had been great sitting in the kitchen with her little man and making cordial early morning conversation. Christine didn't know where that grumpy other person she'd been had gone, but she didn't want her returning any time soon.

When Christine reached the tenth floor, she was surprised to see Ellen standing outside her office door chatting with the secretary. Normally Ellen was nose-to-the-grindstone hard at work by eight o'clock and didn't take a breather until noon.

"Hi, Ellen. Good morning, Sarah," Christine said to the secretary, who gave her a dopey smile. Though she was acting a bit loopy, Christine cut her slack. She was only nineteen and had probably picked up a new boyfriend. This girl traded boyfriends like some people exchanged hasty purchases. Christine used to find it fitting that Sarah was Ellen's secretary, given Ellen's similar penchant for variety. Now, however, it appeared Ellen's shopping days were done.

"Let me just drop my things in my office and I'll be right there," Christine told Ellen as she passed her by.

"Take your time," Ellen said, shooting Sarah a sly smile. "Just don't take too long."

Christine wrinkled her nose, thinking Ellen was acting strange. Did she smell something going on, or was she just imagining it? She dumped her purse, coat, and gloves on the loveseat in her office, and headed back the other way. Sometimes you just didn't know with Ellen. She could be the most wonderful person in the world. But she had a sneaky side, too. Like when she'd broadsided Christine with that vacation in Vermont.

She approached Ellen's office, then suddenly stopped. Both Ellen and Sarah studied her weirdly. Christine turned a suspicious eye on Ellen, and then on Sarah.

"Is something going on?"

"No," Ellen said, a bit too emphatically.

"Not at all!" Sarah chimed in, focusing on her computer.

Just then Christine heard a strange yelp. For the life of her, it sounded like a barking dog. She stared at Ellen, but Ellen just shrugged.

"I don't know," she said mysteriously. "Maybe you should look and see?"

Christine felt her face flash hot. She couldn't possibly mean...?

"Well, go on," Ellen prodded. "Daylight's burning."

Christine laid her hand on the doorknob, every ounce of her tingling from her head to her toes. She shot a quick glance at Ellen, then pressed forward, her heart pounding. It was a vision so surreal she had to blink hard to ensure it wouldn't fade away.

"I must be some kind of absentminded professor," John said, sitting in Ellen's desk chair, Mason perched in his lap. "Because sometimes I forget things. You know, fail to get the details right."

Mason bounded to the floor and happily swaggered over to where Christine stood, dumbstruck. The dog sat expectantly by her side and looked up, wagging his tail. Christine patted his head and stared agape as John rose and walked forward.

"Details?" she asked, her head reeling.

"Like when I put together that business plan."

Christine felt as if she might faint, but was determined that she wouldn't. She had to learn what John was doing here, and why he'd come all this way. It couldn't really be about the paperwork, could it?

"This is about the business plan?" she asked, confused.

John stepped toward her. "I left something pretty important out."

"No, wait," she said, collecting her presence of mind. "John, it was good. I actually read it. And you were right. It's a way to get from A to Z…" She'd nearly forgotten how brilliant his eyes were, their gorgeous blue color offsetting his striking dark hair and handsome face. "Maybe not this year," she continued, "or even the next. In fact, I've figured out that it will take at least five—"

"And naturally, you'll need a nanny."

"A nanny?" she asked as if she hadn't considered it.

"Starting a new business can be very intense. There's no guarantee childcare hours could cover it."

"Well no, maybe not. I haven't thought that far—"

"Perhaps you'd consider a tag-team approach?"

"Tag team?"

"Sure, you know. People do it all the time."

Christine thought quickly, but there was no one around here she could trust to watch Tyler after hours. There was only Ellen and she had her own life, after all. "I don't think Ellen would be willing... What I mean is, that's a lot to ask."

John's lips turned up at the corners as he gave her a longing look. "I wasn't talking about Ellen." He amazed her by pulling her bright red Christmas scarf from behind his back. He now stood just inches away. Christine swallowed hard, her pulse racing. She felt hot, then cold, then warm all over.

"You left this back in Vermont," he said, his voice husky.

"You came all the way to Chicago to return it?"

"For that and something else."

She stared at him, her tender heart daring to hope.

"Christine," he said. "It wasn't until after you'd gone that I realized what an idiot I'd been... what a terrible mess I'd made of everything."

"But I thought you said—"

"Just one more minute. Please hear me out." He shot her a pleading look that sent wild butterflies fluttering inside her. She felt like a child on Christmas morning about to get everything she'd wished for. "I never in a million years expected to meet a woman like you. I mean, I had women friends, sure. But somehow we never... clicked. Then one day this beautiful woman from Chicago nearly ran me off the road. Practically killed me, really."

"Hey!" she protested, but John pressed on.

"But that was nothing next to the near-death I've experienced these past few weeks. I know we have distances to conquer and careers to plan for. But somehow when we're together, everything fits. We're good together, you and I. You, me—and Tyler." Mason barked and John shot him a glance. "And uh, yeah, Mason, too."

Her spirit leapt with joy. She'd tried so hard to push all thoughts of a life with John out of her mind that she hadn't realized how deeply she'd dreamt of one until now.

He draped the scarf around her neck. "Christine, you made me happy too, more happy than I've ever been with anyone. I know I was a jerk in not telling you earlier, and I'm sorry. It just took me time to realize it myself. I had other things that I thought stood in the way, but I was wrong about that too. Please tell me there's still a way to make things right?"

Christine battled the heat in her eyes and forced out the words. "Just what are you saying?"

"That I can't imagine a life without you. I don't *want to* envision my life without you. I believe there's something good here. Something worth fighting for. I think that we stand a chance, Christine, of being together forever. I'm willing to give it my all, if you are. But here's the thing…" He withdrew a small box from his pocket. "I need you with me, you and Tyler both, twenty-four-seven. Day in and day out. Long-distance won't do." John opened the box, exposing a glorious two-carat solitaire. Christine gasped with surprise and met his gaze, her eyes moist.

"I know I haven't done this exactly right," he said, "but I hope you understand my intentions are sincere."

Christine spoke past the lump in her throat. "Yes, yes, I believe you."

He plucked the ring from the box and dropped to one knee as he took her hand.

"I love you desperately, Christine, more desperately than I thought a man could love a woman. Come away with me to Vermont where we can be a family. Where we can build our dreams… But first, tell me you'll be my bride." He slid the ring on her finger and met her eyes with a hopeful gaze. "Say we have a future?"

Christine fought for the words as tears streamed down her face. John was intelligent, loving, and kind. He was just the sort of man she'd always hoped would come and carry her away. Her, and her precious boy too. "The future is long," she said with a shaky smile.

John stood and asked tentatively. "Does that mean yes?"

She nodded and he scooped her into his arms.

"Oh John, I love you too."

"Whoohoo!" he said with a kiss.

Epilogue

Two years later, John set Tyler on his shoulders to crown their Christmas tree with a glistening star. A tiny toboggan ornament sat on a high branch nearby. Christine sighed contentedly, massaging her blooming belly. Last Christmas, they'd shared an intimate mistletoe wedding at Winterhaven. Next year, there'd be another stocking hanging from the mantel and Tyler would have a baby brother or sister. Christine couldn't have imagined a better existence for herself. John was the perfect husband and father, and—with his support—she'd been able to launch her business early. With the New England countryside providing ample inspiration, she'd come up with a number of award-winning designs and her Internet company had taken off, profits skyrocketing. And to think, she owed it all to her pushy best friend who'd insisted she get away to pull her life together.

Christine smiled at Ellen and Carlos, sipping their eggnogs by the fire.

"I'm happy to see you finally broke down and got a Christmas tree," Ellen quipped.

"I had a little help," Christine said, gazing lovingly at John.

"Yeah, and Carlos has offered to help me take it down!"

"I what?" Carlos sputtered, as the rest of the group burst out laughing.

"You lazy old goat," John said, ribbing. "Nobody can get you to do anything at Christmas but eat."

"Oh, I wouldn't say that's exactly true," Ellen said with a mysterious grin.

Christine turned to her, her cheeks flushed with delight. "Ellen?"

Ellen stretched out her left hand and a gemstone glistened on her ring finger.

"Does this mean what I think?" Christine asked with pleased surprise.

Ellen nodded triumphantly.

John put Tyler down and patted Carlos's shoulder. "Way to go, old man!"

"He's not so old," Ellen said, her voice low and sexy.

Carlos turned the color of Santa's suit as Tyler looked cheerily around the room. This was just the Christmas card Christine wanted, she thought as John took her hand. The best part was she got to live it all year through. Tyler hugged Mason and the dog licked his face.

"Merry Christmas, everybody!" the boy said, his cheeks aglow.

Mason barked twice.

The End

A Note from the Author

Thanks for reading *The Christmas Catch*. I hope you enjoyed it. If you did, please help other people find this book.

1. This book is lendable, so loan it to a friend who you think might like it so that she (or he) can discover me, too.

2. Help other people find this book: write a review.

3. Sign up for my newsletter so that that you can learn about the next book as soon as it's available. Write to GinnyBairdRomance@gmail.com with "newsletter" in the subject heading.

4. Come like my Facebook page: http://www.facebook.com/GinnyBairdRomance.

5. Comment on my blog: The Story Behind the Story at http://www.goodreads.com.

6. Visit my website: http://www.ginnybairdromance.com for details on other books available at multiple outlets now.